COCHISE

A MONTANA BOUNTY HUNTERS STORY

DELILAH DEVLIN

ABOUT THE BOOK

Former Army sniper, Cochise Mercier, left Denver SWAT under a cloud of controversy, which was why he ended up back home in Montana, and where he heard about the Montana Bounty Hunters. The "cloud" didn't seem to bother his new boss, so he's all in and finding he enjoys hunting down fugitives for bounties, encumbered by fewer rules.

Sammy McCallister is a by-the-book sheriff's deputy, who has a beef with bounty hunters. Forced to stand by with her gun in her holster, while hunters take down scumbags, she's particularly irked by the new guy in town. Cochise, with his long black hair and thousand-yard-stare makes her uncomfortable, itchy in ways she's never felt before. When she finds herself needing his help, the reason for her irritation becomes all too clear. She wants him. But first, they must make it out of the mountains alive...

CHAPTER 1

Cochise Mercier, the new hire at Montana Bounty Hunters, took a deep breath to force his heart to slow its pace. A trick he'd learned as an Army sniper to make sure a jerking breath didn't mess up a shot. The trick worked in most situations when he needed his mind to slow and for his focus to home in on a target or a situation. Clearing his mind meant he was able to take in more of what was happening around him and enabled him to discard the things that weren't important—like the way the wind beat a tree branch against the side of the house, a steady thump that sounded almost like clomping footsteps. Instead, he concentrated on the way the light, beaming through the tall arched windows at the front of the house, flickered whenever his target paced left or right, telling him where their mark was. An important fact, because in minutes, he'd have to breach the

1

oak front door and be ready to take him down—with his weapon or his body, depending on whether Randy Pinter was armed. A fact Cochise would have to ascertain in a split second.

"Can't see any movement in the back rooms," came Jamie Burke's voice through his earpiece. "I think he's alone."

He still wasn't used to hearing a woman's voice on the comms. He'd never had a female as part of any of his missions on the ground with the Army, and Denver's SWAT had, at the time, been all male. That voice interrupted his calm. His instinct was to protect women and children, but she was a part of this team —and his boss—so again, he drew a deep breath, pushed aside his concern, and concentrated on his target. Pinter was pacing in front of the window to the right of the front door.

"Girlfriend's car isn't in the garage," came Sky Reynold's deep voice. "Must have gone for takeout. I'm moving around to the front."

"Deputies just arrived," Lacey Jones's too perky voice sounded. "I'll go brief them about what's about to go down. Make sure they know we have the owner's permission to be here."

Cochise could hear the excitement in her higher pitch. Thank God, she was back at the road with the vehicles. The thought of her cotton-candy sweetness being anywhere near Pinter made him shudder. The girl might have qualified with her weapon and might

2

be doing well with her self-defense classes, but she had no real experience going head-on with bad dudes. He didn't want to be around the first time she was truly tested.

"You call it, Cochise," Jamie said.

With his heart as slow as when he slept, he felt the familiar ice-water chill flow over him. "Ready," he whispered and then stepped away from the bushes beside the porch. "Moving toward the door... On three. One...two...*three*."

He pounded three times on the door. "Federal Recovery Agent! Get down on the floor!"

Then, just as they'd rehearsed, Sky popped up, used a short cudgel to break the right front window, and tossed a flashbang grenade through the opening he'd made.

Cochise turned his back and crouched beside the door. A split second later, he heard the explosion and a muffled shout. He stood and swung the battering ram against the thick front door. The frame around the door splintered. He tossed the ram and kicked the thick oak, waiting as it slammed forward against dark wood flooring. Then pulling his weapon from its holster, he stepped onto the door into the foyer.

Inside, he saw no sign of Pinter. "Not in foyer. Moving to living room."

"I'm coming your way," Jamie said, and then a moment later, "Mudroom, clear. I'll check the garage."

Sky stepped to the right. "I'll take the kitchen."

Cochise headed through the living room. "Living room clear." Then he moved toward the room farther to the left—a study he'd peered inside earlier. He shoved open the door, stepped to the side, then quickly darted through the opening, bending low as he entered. He glanced behind a sofa, opened the closet. "Clear."

"Clear in the kitchen," said Sky. "Moving toward the stairs."

Cochise cleared the downstairs bathroom, another hallway closet, and then ran up the stairs. Just as he reached the darkened landing, he saw Sky back out of a bedroom and shake his head. Cochise signaled that he'd head right toward what he suspected was the master bedroom, while Sky took a smaller bedroom at the other end of the hallway. Cochise unclipped his Maglite from his web belt and shone it down the darkened hallway.

"Garage clear," Jamie said.

"Make sure the bastard didn't circle around to the backyard." Lacey and Dagger had the road and yard fence line covered, and both were quiet.

Just as he reached out to turn the door handle for the master bedroom, Sky whispered, "Clear." Cochise tensed. Last possible place.

Pinter must have shot up the steps the second the window was broken. Slippery bastard. Something they'd learned talking to the cops who'd arrested him for a home invasion. The fact the judge had awarded him bail after he'd led the police on a three-mile foot race through backyards, over fences, and through busy intersections, where he'd nearly lost the cops, had the entire team shaking their heads. The $500,000 bail must have seemed an impossible goal for a two-time loser, but the prosecutor hadn't looked closely enough at the family to raise an argument. They hadn't known the grandfather doted on the prick. He'd willingly used his ranch to secure the bond.

Why Pinter had chosen a life of crime was beyond Cochise. He came from money, dated money, and now, he was facing decades in jail after beating up a couple he'd robbed at gunpoint for a measly sixty dollars and a wedding ring.

Sky came up beside him, a shotgun loaded with beanbag rounds raised, with the stock against his shoulder, and cupping a flashlight against the barrel. He gave Cochise a nod.

Cochise quietly turned the knob then shoved it open. Sky preceded him through the door, turning his body to the left then the right.

Cochise went to the bed and flipped the mattress off the frame. Nobody huddled under it. He quietly slid open the nightstand drawer, the place where Mr. Anderson said he kept a handgun. Shining the light inside the drawer, Cochise noted it was empty, except for a bag of cough drops and loose change. Catching Sky's glance, he shook his head.

He moved to the bathroom door while Sky sped to the walk-in closet.

As he turned the handle, he heard the scuff of a foot and froze. Withdrawing his hand, he signaled to Sky, who quickly edged to the opposite side of the door.

Pinter had plenty of warning they were there. He had no place left to hide. Likely had the gun. Cochise's best route would be to get him to surrender.

"Randy," Cochise called out, "you're not getting out of this house. We're bounty hunters, and we've been tracking you for days. A whole goddamn team to take down your sorry ass. We have deputies in the road out front in case you decide to be stupid. You're not going to be stupid, are you?"

Sky moved a step backward. "We think we have him cornered in the upstairs bathroom," he whispered to the team. "Get eyes on the side of the house beneath the window."

"Already there," Dagger said.

Sky moved closer.

"Buddy," Cochise said, keeping an even tone. "Your best move is to come out with your hands up where we can see them."

Ten seconds passed. Not a sound came from behind the closed door.

Again, Cochise reached out and gripped the knob. It was locked. Stepping in front of the door, he raised a foot.

But he heard a click and pitched to the side. An explosion ripped through the door.

On his back on the floor, Cochise stared at a circle with splintered edges right where he'd been standing a second earlier. He rolled to his feet, his weapon aimed at the hole.

"What the fuck?" Jamie shouted in his ear. "Coming up the stairs."

"Deputies are running for the house," Lacey said sounding breathless, like she was running, too.

In the distance, he heard several sets of footsteps stomping quickly up the stairs. No way was he letting the women anywhere near this vicious pig. He aimed at the door. "Better get on the ground, Pinter." Then he fired two shots, just to make sure the dirtbag was taking cover, and kicked in the door.

Inside the room, he made out the glint of metal coming from around the side of the shower stall. He ducked into the stall as a shot was fired. Then he darted out again, reaching out his left hand as the handgun appeared around the corner. With his back to Pinter, he gripped the weapon, shoving it, and the hand that held it, to the side. A bullet hit the toilet, shattering porcelain. Water spilled out onto the floor.

A punch landed against his ribs, knocking the breath from his lungs, but Cochise didn't let go of the gun, he spun and shoved the hand holding the gun against the edge of the stall.

The gun clattered away.

More punches hit his sides—much good that did,

because his Kevlar vest took the blows—but Cochise couldn't end this while all he held was Pinter's hand. He jerked Pinter forward then backed him into the shower stall, crushing him against the tile with his body, unable to turn because he still held his own weapon outstretched. With his elbow, he beat backwards, catching Pinter in his sides.

Searing pain in the corner of his shoulder sucked away what was left of his breath. "Motherfucker, did you bite me?"

He beat back his elbow and aimed a backward kick at a knee.

The lights to the bathroom flashed on.

Sky filled the doorway, his glance taking in the gun on the floor. He moved forward and reached out. Gladly, Cochise gave him his weapon, and then turned and pummeled Pinter, clipping him in the jaw, the ribs, then giving him another punch to the jaw.

As Randy Pinter sagged toward the gray stone floor of the shower, Cochise kept his fists balled. But Pinter's eyelids lowered, and his jaw relaxed.

A clap against his shoulder made him wince. "Think we have him," Sky said.

Cochise lowered his eyebrows. "We?"

Sky grinned. "Hey, I freed your hand."

"Fucker."

"Tell me that wasn't satisfying."

Cochise grunted.

Just then, Jamie rounded the corner, two deputies

crowding in behind her. One tall, burly male and a female with scraped-back, blondish hair and angry eyes.

Suddenly, the spacious bathroom was too crowded.

"Do we have to call an ambulance?" Jamie asked.

Sky leaned over Pinter and ran his hands over his body, doing a quick search for weapons. When he straightened, he aimed a kick at his hip.

Pinter stirred and moaned.

"Nope, he's conscious," Sky said, his mouth curving into a smirk. "Jail's just fifteen minutes away. They can take him to the ER to be checked out."

Cochise bent and rested his hands on his knees, dragging in deep breaths to clear his head of the anger still pounding through him.

Jamie came up beside him and plucked at the neck of his tee. "Too bad he didn't get a mouthful of Kevlar. That has to hurt. Buddy, you might need stiches. Sky and I will make sure this one gets to jail, and that they know to test Pinter for any nasty diseases. Your vehicle's still back at the office; I can have Lacey take you to the ER."

Cochise straightened, inwardly cursing the fact his truck was back at the agency parking lot. He'd ridden with Sky and Jamie on the way over.

"I'd love to," Lacey said, her blonde head peering around the corner, "but I can't wait on you. Dagger and I have to drive to Whitefish to meet up with Reaper. He texted that he may have found Wallace's hideout." She gave a hundred-watt smile. "We're riding into the mountains on horseback."

Jamie groaned. "Good Lord. Last time Reaper was on horseback, he nearly drowned in a stock pond."

"You can drop me at my truck. I can get myself to the ER," Cochise said, and warmed to the idea. Anything to avoid listening to Dagger give Bounty Hunter Barbie another long lesson about how not to get killed doing her job. "You two need to get on the road, or you won't get any rest."

A throat cleared to his right. The female deputy's frown was fierce, but she lifted her chin. "I can drop you, but I won't wait around."

He nodded. From her expression, she was about as thrilled with the idea as he was. She'd dump him at the entrance, and he'd be on his own. The way he liked it. "Suits me fine. And I appreciate it."

* * *

The bite took seven small stitches. With a script for amoxicillin, and a sample-sized tube of antibiotic cream and gauze pads in his pocket, he strode toward the hospital entrance. Once outside, he'd find a bench and call an Uber or Brian Cobb, who lived in the apartment at the back of the agency's offices.

However, when he stepped outside into the early morning sunshine, Officer McCallister, the female cop who'd delivered him to the ER, was standing there, leaning against the door of her squad car.

He slowed his steps. "You waiting on me?"

"Nope, but I was in the area and checked with the ER desk. They said you were on your way out..." Her light brown eyebrows nearly met in the middle. "Do you want a ride or not?"

His lips twitched. "Not a morning person?"

Her green eyes narrowed. "I'll drop you at Montana Bounty Hunters. That's the end of my good deeds. My shift ends in half an hour."

He opened the passenger side door and slid onto the bench seat. Once there, he stretched out his arm across the back and leaned against the door. His shoulder ached like fire. The doctor had recommended ibuprofen for the pain, but he had a bottle of tequila chilling in the fridge that would work just fine.

"Seatbelt?"

He grimaced and reached to secure his belt. Then he settled back against his door again. The better to scope out Officer McCallister. "Name's Cochise Mercier," he said, deciding someone needed to be polite.

"I know who you are."

And he waited. When she didn't reciprocate with an introduction, he cleared his throat. "I haven't been in Bear Lodge that long, but you know who I am..."

Her gaze went to her rearview mirror than back to the windshield. "Sheriff likes to keep tabs on everyone working at MBH." She shot him a quick glance. "You were with Denver SWAT. Must have fucked up bad to wind up here."

He barely suppressed a grunt of surprise at her blunt words. But he had fucked up. Still, he wasn't unhappy about the change of place or pace of his current circumstances. A man could breathe here— crisp mountain air, without the traffic and mass of humanity. "Yeah," he said, not willing to get into it with a woman who seemed ready to pick a fight. "Something like that."

"Should have applied for a patrol job. Sheriff's always looking for officers with experience. He'd overlook a lot."

"Thanks for the suggestion, but I like what I'm doing now, and the money's better."

Again, her gaze cut his way, and that frown dug a line between her eyes.

"You don't like bounty hunters."

"Didn't say that."

"Didn't have to." He eyed her profile—stubborn chin, cute nose, freckles on her pale cheeks. Her hair was a dark blonde with glints of red as the dawn's light struck it. Her body was sturdy—not too slim, muscled. He doubted she'd like that description, but he liked a strong woman. "You got a first name, Officer McCallister?" he asked, still watching her and knowing he was making her a little uncomfortable, because her eyebrows remained lowered.

Or maybe that was her permanent expression.

Again, his mouth twitched.

"Samantha."

"Sammy," he drawled.

"My friends call me Sammy."

This time, he let the smile creep across his mouth.

Just as they were nearing the turn that would take them to the agency, a car pulled out from a side street, nearly clipping the squad car.

Officer McCallister hit the brakes then cussed under her breath.

He knew the feeling. This close to ending a shift and some asshole forces a decision.

When the blue Taurus swerved into the center of the road, she sighed and reached for the toggle, turning on her blue lights.

The car indicated to the right and pulled onto the shoulder of the road.

"Stay in the car," she said, not looking toward Cochise.

He watched with interest as she approached the vehicle, keeping at a safe angle as she neared the car. She reached for the radio on her shoulder. "Dispatch, I need you to run a plate." She gave the dispatcher the plate information while he listened to the radio inside the car.

A few seconds later, dispatch responded. "The car's registered to Loretta Mackinaw. She has an outstanding warrant for possession of a controlled substance."

The officer's body tensed.

Cochise rolled down his window to listen as she shouted for the driver to put her hands on the dash.

The first hint there was trouble was Officer McCallister flicking the strap on her holster and drawing her gun. A shot rang out, and she dove beside the car.

Cochise slid across the bench, lifting his legs to get past the equipment blocking his way, and settled into the driver's seat just as the Taurus pulled out onto the road, a black cloud gusting from the exhaust pipe.

Putting the squad car in drive, he pulled up beside the officer and shouted through the open window, "Get in!"

She didn't argue, sliding into the passenger side seat, flipping on the siren, and reaching for the radio. "Dispatch. Shots fired. I'm in pursuit of that blue Taurus." She gave her location while Cochise concentrated on keeping on Mackinaw's tail.

"You okay?" he asked, not taking his gaze off the car ahead.

"Missed me. Not that she meant to."

They passed the outskirts of town and entered the open highway.

"Just thirty fucking minutes," she muttered.

"How long do we follow?" he asked, wondering if they'd run up against the county line and pass the problem to the next jurisdiction.

"There's a crossroads up ahead. Open. No trees

or buildings. Think you can get close enough to perform a PIT maneuver?" She cussed again. "Goddamn, I should be behind the wheel. Sheriff'll have my ass."

He grinned and gunned the accelerator, closing the distance between the vehicles. Further down the road, he saw the crossroads, no other vehicles in sight. "Let's do it."

Another punch of gas, and he pulled into the left lane. Coming even with the left rear wheel of the Taurus, he turned into the car, giving it a solid slam. The Taurus began to spin left, and Cochise braked, slowing the car to watch as the Taurus continued its spin and took out the stop sign across the intersection before coming to a halt. The driver faced them through the windshield.

All Cochise saw was frizzy mud-brown hair and a red face.

Officer McCallister toggled the loudspeaker and raised her mic. "Loretta, put your hands on the dashboard."

The woman complied, although her frown didn't abate.

Officer McCallister gave him a quick glance. "There's a rifle in the trunk. Key's on the ring."

He gave a nod, turned off the engine, and let himself out of the car, making sure to keep the driver's side door open as a shield. He retrieved the rifle and returned, crouching behind the door. He glanced across the empty seat to where the female officer stood, crouching behind her open door. She finished calling in a request for backup, and then her gaze met his across the expanse.

"Whatever move you want to make," he said, "I have your back."

CHAPTER 2

Sᴀᴍᴍʏ ʟᴏᴏᴋᴇᴅ up from the report she was filling out to stare through the glass window of the sheriff's small office. Cochise had been seated in front of his desk for the past forty minutes. Voices were muffled, so the sheriff had settled down a bit since he'd arrived at the crossroads to find a bounty hunter holding a rifle pointed at Loretta Mackinaw as she lay on her belly, bleeding from a gunshot wound to her thigh while Sammy applied pressure to the wound.

The shot had been precise, embedding in fleshy meat, all major blood vessels missed.

She remembered the moment he'd looked across that leather bench seat and said, *Whatever move you want to make...*

Good Lord, he'd taken away her breath. The fact he was beautiful—sharp, high cheekbones, red-brown skin, eyes so dark they were almost black...well, that was only the beginning of what made her so aware of him. Also enticing was the inky dark hair that he scraped so negligently back in a ponytail that hit him between the shoulder blades, like he was growing it out.

Holy fuck, she remembered the first time she'd seen him. In Gladys Morton's bakery on Main Street, or rather leaving the bakery as she'd been parked across the street. Her hand had been on the door latch, and she'd frozen the moment he'd walked out, squinted up into the sunshine, and then slid shades over his eyes. His body was perfect—tall, broad shoulders, well-sculpted arms, lean waist. She'd been ready to run his plates just to find his address—strictly against the rules, but she might have, if she hadn't noticed he exited with Dagger Renfrew, someone she knew worked at Montana Bounty Hunters.

Once she'd confirmed with the sheriff that they had a new hunter in town, she'd grudgingly put a brake on her interest. Bounty hunters were cowboys —dangerous ones, who didn't like rules and didn't play well with others. She couldn't count the number of times she'd sat in her patrol car, while hunters broke into homes on some flimsy excuse for probable cause to take down a bad guy. In her opinion, they loved the chase, didn't care who got hurt in the process, and counted their ill-gotten gain all the way to the bank, while police officers had to follow the rules, *to the freaking letter*, or their careers were toast.

Still, she was grateful Cochise had been there today. After she'd gotten Loretta out of the car and moving toward the center of the highway with her hands held high, Sammy had moved away from her door, her weapon pointed at the woman. When she'd given Loretta the order to go to her knees, the woman had given her a small, cold smile and reached behind her neck.

Cochise dropped her the second he'd seen the glint of metal in her hand. Her own reflexes hadn't been that quick. And he'd done it without killing the woman. Even though he wasn't deputized in this state, he'd followed the rules and made the right call. He might also have saved her life, or at least, saved her from making a shot she'd have to live with for the rest of her days.

Sammy hoped the sheriff saw it that way, too, and that he wouldn't fire her for giving Cochise her weapon.

Yes, this was Montana, and the sheriff's office wasn't some big city department where everyone covered their asses to prevent lawsuits, but an officer of the law was expected to hold true to certain rules.

The door opened, and Cochise strode toward her desk. "Suppose it's too much to ask..."

She fought a begrudging smile. He already thought she was the biggest bitch. Best to keep him at a distance. "Let me check with the sheriff to see if he needs anything else."

He nodded, and she slipped into the Sheriff Miller's office. She slid her report across his desk, and then waited for him to glance up.

His gaze narrowed on her. Same look he always gave her. She was the first female deputy he'd ever hired. She supposed he might have felt like he had to and resented the fact. He hadn't exactly been welcoming. Eight months in, and she still waited for a sign he approved of the job she was doing.

He sat back in his chair and drummed his fingers on his desk. His gaze remained on her, and she stood still, hands planted in the middle of her lower back while she waited for him to say whatever he was going to say.

His lips pursed, and then he gave her a nod. "Good call back there. Your instincts, trusting that hunter..." He nodded again. "Good call. Now, get out of here."

She went to attention then turned on her heel and left his office. Once outside, her eyebrows rose. What the hell had just happened? Was he happy she'd trusted *a man* to take the shot? She didn't know whether to laugh or be pissed.

Cochise straightened from where he'd been leaning against her desk. "Everything okay?"

She nodded and grabbed the keys to her truck. "I'll give you that lift."

Once outside on the sidewalk, he touched her sleeve. "You had her, you know. You didn't need me there."

"I know." And she smiled.

His gaze flickered over her mouth then back up. The corners of his eyes wrinkled. "I'll follow you," he said, waving an arm for her to lead the way.

A man who had her back. Who didn't think he'd had to be there to "save" her.

Easy, Sammy, she warned herself. Just because he was easy on the eyes and knew his way around a rifle didn't mean she could let down her guard. He was a bounty hunter. One day, they'd wind up on opposite sides of a bad situation. "We're here," she said, grimacing because she knew her truck looked like a POS.

Twenty years had passed since the new car smell had faded. Most days, Sammy didn't give a rat's ass what anyone thought of her wheels. She'd inherited the truck from her dad, knew all its foibles, had changed out most of what was under the hood, other than the engine. So, the old Chevy had some miles on her, she still rumbled like a tiger.

She pointed at the passenger-side door. "You have to lift it while you pull the handle..."

Turning on her heel, she went around the truck and climbed into the driver's seat. When she turned the key, she smiled at the way it purred. So, the engine was too loud for her to ever enjoy her radio, but the truck was paid for. It had personality. Sammy tapped the dashboard, as was her habit, a good luck gesture her dad had always made, and dropped the gear stick into reverse.

Ten minutes later, she pulled into the parking lot in front of Montana Bounty Hunters.

Cochise climbed down and stared across at her. "See you around, Samantha."

She wrinkled her nose. "Sammy."

His dark eyes sparkled, and he lifted his chin. Then he turned and walked away.

She found it strange that the sunlight dimmed as he left her. Suddenly, her long night's shift weighed on her body. She hadn't felt tired for a second when he'd been with her. Sammy shook her head and moved the gearshift into drive, and then picked up her phone and hit the first number on her speed dial list.

As soon as she heard the voice on the other end sleepily say, "Hello," she said, "Need me to pick up anything for breakfast?"

Her sister groaned. "You woke me up for that?"

"Time to get up, lazy butt. You've got work in an hour."

"No, I don't. Remember, I have two days off? Brady and I are going camping in Kootenai."

Sammy made a face. She'd forgotten about her little sis's "grownup" vacation. Brady was all right. At least, he had a clean rap sheet. But her sister could do better. She was heading to college in the Fall. Sammy's worry was that her sister would change her mind about going, because she thought she was in love with the young man who worked on one of the area's ranches. A real cowboy with no prospects. Not that Sammy was a snob. But she was a realist. She didn't want her sister to always have to work hard. They'd had enough of that life. Once Sheri had college out of the way, Sammy would breathe easier. If, by then, her sister still wanted the cowboy, well at least she could make it on her own. She'd have her own set of prospects.

Sammy was ready to let go of the apron strings. Ready to concentrate on living her own life. She'd played mom to her kid sister for the past nine years since their parents had died after being stranded on the road during a blizzard. She hadn't needed a college degree to get into the police academy, and the pay and the respect that came with the job sure beat the hell out of waiting tables. She wasn't sure what she wanted to be when she "grew up", but school was still in the back of her mind.

However, there was no use dreaming about it now. She needed sleep before Brady showed up. Then she'd give him "the talk" about keeping her kid sister safe, and she'd make sure both of them had plenty of condoms. Sheri was sure to throw a fit, but again, Sammy was just being real.

* * *

After Cochise heard Sammy's truck pull away, he wished he could've thought of a reason to delay her leaving. He could have invited her in for a cup of coffee. Maybe asked her to breakfast. Or asked her out on a date. She'd have turned him down cold, but he'd have enjoyed watching the fire flash in her eyes and her brows draw into another fierce frown.

"Hey!"

Cochise glanced toward Jamie, who sat beside Brian as they reviewed their daily list of available bounties. He sauntered their way, wishing he hadn't left his keys in his desk, or he would've been five minutes away from his bed.

As he drew near, Jamie shook her head. "Heard about your adventure this morning."

His glance went to the police scanner sitting on the corner of Brian's desk.

Brian grinned. "Thought I was hearing things when your voice called for an ambulance."

Jamie folded her arms over her chest. "Do I need to worry about you jumping ship to join the sheriff's office?"

He grunted. "Hell, no. Told you when you hired me, I'm done with departments. Done with the politics. I like this work just fine." And although he had to fight a yawn first, he asked, "Anything interesting?" and aimed his chin toward the list displayed on the monitor.

Jamie's face screwed up. "There are some easy jobs. But there's one..." She shook her head. "I still can't believe the judge let this guy out on the street..."

She clicked on a link and brought up an arrest warrant, then she turned the monitor toward him, and he leaned down to read the name. *Luke Ford.*

The picture was of a man in his early thirties, shaved head, dead eyes. Cochise had lived here long enough to know most of the worst criminals in the area, and Luke Ford was a whole different category of shithead. In his twenties, he'd attacked his girlfriend when she was leaving him, cutting the tendons at the backs of her heels to keep her from getting away. He'd done ten measly years for the assault. The jury had been convinced by his attorney that a man couldn't rape his girlfriend, so that charge had been dismissed. Didn't matter he'd mutilated her to make sure he could have her.

Ten years had turned into seven, and he hadn't been out on the streets three months before he'd assaulted another woman. But the same judge who'd sat on his criminal trial had granted bail. Now, Ford was in the wind.

From the look on Jamie's face, she was feeling like he was. Luke Ford didn't belong walking free. Hell, as far as Cochise was concerned, he didn't deserve to exist. The bounty was worth a cool twenty thousand, although Cochise would have done it for free. He met Jamie's gaze. "We're going after him, right?"

"Yeah. I wish more of the team was here."

"No new hires? I'm tired of being the probie," he muttered and arched an eyebrow.

Brian cleared his throat. "A friend of mine has already applied. He was Army, same as you. And he was a Ranger, so not a lightweight."

"He starting today?" Cochise asked, glancing at the boss.

Jamie was already reaching for the phone. "I should probably tell you a thing or two about him..."

"Just get him here. I need to head home to shower and clear my head. I'll be back in an hour."

With a new sense of purpose, Cochise headed out the door. Another day, another scumbag. Best part of his job was delivering the bastards straight to jail. He'd take great satisfaction in dropping Luke Ford in a cage. He couldn't stand men who got their kicks hurting women. He didn't understand the appeal. There had to be something dark and twisted in a man's soul to hurt someone he professed to love.

He'd never been in love but couldn't imagine ever getting so enraged with a woman he'd want to savage her. People like Ford made his belly boil. Made him want to "take the shot" whether or not he had the right. Which was why he was in Montana and not still in Denver. He'd taken out the bad guy after being ordered to stand down.

But he had no regrets. Pedro Gonzalez had already killed the bank's security guard. He'd threatened to kill the bank manager if he didn't get a ride to the airport. Like he'd actually believed they'd give him a plane to fly back to Mexico.

Cochise was sitting on the rooftop across from the bank, staring down the scope as Gonzalez raised his weapon and signaled for the manager to come closer. "Chief, I've got the shot," he said into his mic.

"Good to know, Mercier. But hold on."

Cochise cussed under his breath. Gonzalez was already agitated as hell. A simple robbery had been spoiled by the security guard who'd halted him just inside the bank's door. As soon as Gonzalez had pulled his weapon and shot the guard, someone inside the bank had hit the silent alarm. Three minutes later, squad cars arrived, and he'd been trapped inside. Another five, and SWAT had rolled in.

Looking down his scope, he saw Gonzalez's lips lift in a snarl, and his finger slid toward the trigger of the gun. He'd already promised there would be blood. A killing for every ten minutes he had to wait for his ride. Cochise drew a slow breath, slowed his heart, and took the shot.

The review board had been sympathetic. Praised his military record. Didn't lament Gonzalez's death one bit. But Cochise had disobeyed an order. Simple as that.

He'd remained stoic throughout the hearing. His attorney had laid out all the possible actions they could take, including bringing him up on charges, but the lawyer had said he should be happy if they settled for firing him. He didn't have a chance in hell of being reinstated.

Cochise had no regrets. Just like he had none about shooting the woman this morning. She was still alive. Maybe next time, she'd think twice about drawing on a cop.

Just outside of Bear Lodge, he turned onto the gravel road that led to his isolated home. He pulled up beside the house, cut the engine, and sat for a few minutes, letting his head fall back against the headrest. No time for sleep. He'd shower, check his "go bag", and head back out. Luke Ford was out there. The women in this part of the state weren't safe. No way could he sit back and hit pause because he was tired.

Not when every victim wore his sister's face.

He let himself out of his Expedition and walked the pea-gravel path to his porch. He made a face at the peeling paint. At least, the windows were no longer yellow with grime. He ought to just hire a contractor to finish out the place, but he'd wanted a project to keep him busy in his off hours. He just hadn't counted on there being so much work, or the agency throwing him in the deep end so quickly.

He unlocked his door and made a mental note to himself to hit the post office before he headed back to the agency, so he could pick up his mail. Not that he expected any letters from friends or family. He had none—other than his hereditary relationship with the Blackfoot Nation—not that he knew a soul on the reservation, but he had felt a sense of "coming home" when he'd chosen Montana as the next place he'd hang his hat.

He sniffed the air then walked around the living room, lifting windows to let in a fresh breeze. Then he moved to the kitchen and pulled open the door to the cabinet beneath the sink. Last Monday's takeout was the source of the sour smell. He pulled the bag from the trashcan and walked it outside, but the trashcans there were full. He'd missed trash pick-up day. *Fucking hell.* He placed the bag in the back of his truck. He'd dispose of it inside the bin behind the agency.

After stripping, he carried his dirty clothes to the laundry room, filled the washing machine, but he didn't start it. When the hell would he back to transfer the load to the dryer? He'd have another smell to deal with when he got back, after they got Ford.

Cochise set the coffeemaker to brew a fresh pot and hit the shower. However, he had to traipse back to the laundry room to restart the water heater. Fuck, he didn't have time to wait for hot water, so he took a cold shower, which at least woke him up. With fresh clothes, a repacked bag, and hot coffee in a thermos, he headed back out the door.

He hadn't been this tired since he'd been a private going through basic training. At thirty-seven, he was beginning to feel his age. A yawn caught him by surprise, but he didn't slow his steps.

He remembered he'd left windows open but shrugged. He didn't have anything inside worth stealing. Thieves could have his TV. He rarely had time to watch it anyway. His photographs were the only things he treasured, and they wouldn't mean anything to anyone but him.

Inside his truck, he flipped down his visor and stared at the photo of his sister. He smoothed a gentle fingertip over her face. "Hey, sis. Still thinking of you." Then he flipped up the visor, despite the fact the morning sun stung his eyes. Maria's dark gaze and wide smile always hurt his heart.

CHAPTER 3

AT THE END of her next shift, Sammy tried her sister's cellphone number again. She wasn't particularly alarmed when the call went straight to voice mail. The kids were camping in the Kootenai National Forest near Eureka. They'd warned her cell reception would be poor.

Before they'd left, Brady had put her mind at ease, explaining he had plenty of experience hunting and hiking there, because his family went several times a year to the area he'd shown her on the map.

Still, she was a little annoyed she couldn't reach her sister. Checking on her was an ingrained habit.

Sammy lowered her phone. She was tired but edgy. And hungry. Deciding some fresh kolaches from the Bear Lodge Bakery were just what she needed, she turned onto Main Street and parked her truck right in front—one of the advantages of being up this time of morning. As she approached the bakery, she glanced through the window. Gladys was already serving a customer fresh coffee and goodies. The bell above the door tinkled as she pushed inside.

She instantly recognized the blonde at the counter, or rather, the Malinois seated on the ground beside her. "Hey, Tessa," Sammy said as she approached. Tessa and her handler, Jamie Burke, were well-known in the area, since Tessa was often called to search for missing kids and hikers. Although a bounty hunter, Sammy gave Jamie a pass because she was so friendly, and her service dog was a local hero.

Jamie glanced to her side and gave Sammy a smile. "Mornin'. You just get off shift?"

Sammy nodded. "Heading home. Needed sustenance first." She glanced at the big box of kolaches Gladys was closing on the counter. "Hope you didn't scarf them all up."

Jamie laughed. "I have plenty. You should drop by the office. Brian has fresh coffee made."

Sammy opened her mouth to give an automatic pass on the invitation, but then wondered whether Cochise would be around. It was early, so probably not, but she'd never been inside the agency and was curious. "You sure you have enough?"

Jamie's grin widened, and she turned back to the wiry, gray-haired woman behind the counter. "Gladys, add a few more. We're having company."

Sammy felt foolish as she followed Jamie back to her office. Several vehicles were parked in front, including one silver Expedition. Her heart began to thud, and her palms grew moist. "Jesus, he's going to think I'm stalking him," she muttered. As she stepped down to the pavement, she felt a blush heat her cheeks.

Inside, she glanced around. A long low counter separated a reception area from a large bullpen filled with several desks.

Jamie walked around the counter and glanced back. "Don't be shy now. Follow me."

Sammy shook her head and trailed behind her to a kitchen area that had a large table and a counter filled with a microwave and a commercial-sized Bunn coffeemaker.

"All the comforts of home," Jamie said, sliding the pastry box onto the table. "Grab a cup of coffee. You must be dead on your feet. I'll go roust the guys and let them know we have food. We pulled another all-nighter, and they caught a nap while I fetched breakfast."

Sammy searched the cupboard and found a coffee cup. She stood sipping the dark brew when Brian Cobb rolled inside in his wheelchair.

His dark eyebrows shot upward. "Morning, deputy. Heard you and Cochise had some excitement yesterday."

Sammy shrugged. "He was a huge help."

He waggled his eyebrows. "We try to be good citizens. Mind handing me a cup? I could sneak one from the dishwasher, but you're in the way."

Sammy blinked, not sure if he was irritated with her or teasing, but she hurried to the cupboard and got him a cup. She even poured the coffee. When she handed it to him, he winked.

With another blush suffusing her cheeks, she glanced up to see Cochise stride through the door.

His gaze locked with hers, and he paused in the doorway. "The sheriff need something from me?"

Coming up behind him, Jamie laughed and clapped his shoulder. "No, I bought all the kolaches, so I invited her to have breakfast with us."

Cochise's eyes narrowed a fraction, and his gaze trailed over her face. "Any more excitement last night?"

She shook her head. "No bounty hunters shooting up the place..." She bit her lip. Maybe not the nicest thing she could have said inside their own house, but old habits die hard.

"Have a seat," Jamie said. "Sky's grabbing a shower. Have you met my fiancé? He should be along any minute now."

Sammy shook her head.

Jamie sat and waved a hand at the box. "Please, better grab a few before they're gone. These guys can eat."

Relieved to have something to do, she took a seat and helped herself to three of the sausage-stuffed pastries. "Anything exciting happening in your world?" she asked as she took her first bite.

The three of them shared charged glances, which heightened her curiosity.

Brian wrinkled his nose. "We've been tracking a skip. Luke Ford."

Sammy blinked. "He didn't make his court date?" She knew well who the creep was, but he wasn't from Bear Lodge, so he wasn't on her radar.

"Nope, he's in the wind." Brian raked a hand through his shaggy brown hair. "We spent the last day and night trying to get a bead on where he's at. I've been making calls to old employers and girl-friends, who are mostly freaked out about the fact he's a ghost. These guys," he said, tipping his head toward Jamie and Cochise, "were up in Libby. He dumped his car in town. His family has property just north of there and a cabin up on a lake."

Jamie reached for a pastry. "We spoke with his cousin last night. He said he thinks Ford will make a run for the border. He's spent a lot of time hunting around Eureka, so he knows the area well. From there, it's just a long hike to Canada."

A wave of dizziness swept over Sammy, and she dropped her pastry to the table.

"You okay?" Cochise said. "You went white."

"It's a big area...Eureka," she said, realizing her breaths had shortened.

"Sammy?"

She hadn't realized Jamie had left her chair and was kneeling beside her. Maybe she was dizzy because she was tired. Her mind was working slow.

"My sister and her boyfriend are in Kootenai. Hiking."

"It's a lot of forest," Brian said, his voice soft. "Chances of them meeting..."

"Slim. I know." Sammy pushed on the table to stand, but she swayed.

The next second, she felt herself swinging upward.

Cochise held her in his arms. "There's a couch in Brian's room. You need to lie down for a minute."

"A minute," she parroted. Her sister was in the forest. The same forest where Luke Ford might be. "I have to go."

"Not now, you don't."

From her vantage, she noted the sharp edge of his strong jaw. A muscle flexed along that line. He carried her easily, although she knew she wasn't light. "Sorry. Not usually such a wimp," she said.

"Your sister's out there," Jamie said, from somewhere behind them. "I'd be freaking out, too."

The whir of wheels sounded from in front of them. A door opened. Cochise lowered her to a soft surface, and then took a knee beside her. His expression was grim. "We're going to find him."

"It's a big area..." she repeated.

"If you're worried," Jamie said, holding out a wet cloth, which Cochise took and lay against her forehead, "you can come with us."

Come with them? Bounty hunters? But then her mind clicked. They were hunting Ford. At least, she'd be part of a team. They'd cover more ground than she could alone... "I have a couple of days off..."

"Call the sheriff," Jamie said. "Tell him what's happening."

She nodded and dragged the cloth from her forehead. She needed to go home and change. Pack. Get her shit together. She shifted and sat up, clutching the cloth. Her stomach clenched, and she worried for a second that she'd deepen her embarrassment by vomiting. "She's all the family I have."

"I understand," Cochise said. "We'll find her. Then we'll find Ford." His glance cut to Jamie, who nodded.

"What's your sister's name?" Jamie asked.

"Sheri. She's eighteen."

Cochise swallowed. "I'll drive you home, so you can get packed."

"I can drive myself," she said frowning.

He shook his head.

Sammy rolled her eyes. Not a good move. She flattened her hand against her stomach. "Okay, but I might have to pull over on the way."

He stood and held out his hand.

Although she wished she didn't need the help, she clasped his hand and let him pull her up. He held tight to her hand for few seconds, but when she proved she could stand without nearly fainting this time, he moved back.

"If you don't mind me riding along..." she said, glancing at Jamie.

"We'd be glad to have you." Her glance shifted to Cochise. "While you're gone, we'll pull up maps and print out everything we have so far on Ford."

He gave a crisp nod and cupped Sammy's elbow.

A gesture she appreciated, because she felt stronger when he touched her. Somehow reassured. She should be worried about that.

* * *

They took Cochise's vehicle to her apartment. He walked up the concrete steps with their iron railing, following her only a step behind. After she let them both inside, he stood near the door and glanced around at the photographs on the counter dividing the kitchen from the living room. "This your sister?" he said, moving forward and picking up a framed photo.

Sammy glanced at the picture of her sister, smiling with sunshine lighting up her blonde hair. She wore a pink sundress and a stack of pretty cord bracelets in a rainbow of colors on her wrist. "Yes, that was taken this year. We should take that. In case..." A shiver traveled across her skin.

"You go get changed and packed. I'll call the sheriff."

She frowned, a little irritated with the fact he was taking over again. "You two best buddies now?"

His expression gave away nothing of his thoughts. "He's a good man. He'll want to know."

She nodded and trudged toward her bathroom.

"Sammy."

She glanced over her shoulder.

"Get something of your sister's, something with her scent."

She sucked in a breath and nodded.

After taking a quick shower, she dressed then brushed her wet hair and put it in a ponytail where it dripped on the back of her T-shirt. She dragged a duffel from under her bed and filled it with the bare-essential toiletries and clothing—jeans, tees, a light jacket, underwear, and socks. Then she went to her gun safe and placed her service pistol inside and took out her personal weapon, a Springfield in a holster, checking the magazine and grabbing a box of rounds. She added them to the duffel along with her phone charger.

Then she headed to her sister's room. It wasn't hard to find something rich with her sister's smell. Sheri hadn't done laundry in a week. Sammy took an old tee from her hamper, wrapped it in a plastic bag, and stuffed that inside her duffel, too.

When she returned to the living room, Cochise was standing in the same place she'd left him. His glance went to her bag, and he held out his hand. Suppressing the urge to tell him she was perfectly capable of carrying her own shit, she handed it over. He held open the door for her and followed her back to the SUV, where he stowed her duffel in the back.

"You got your wallet?" he asked as he slid into the front seat.

"And my badge," she quipped.

He turned the key and flipped down his visor, and then did something that made her breath hitch. He touched a photo clipped to the back of the visor, caressing the cheek of a pretty young girl with dark eyes and skin. She looked so much like him, Sammy knew they had to be related. So, he did understand about sisters.

She settled back in her seat.

"Seatbelt?" He raised an eyebrow, and one side of his mouth lifted.

Giving him a small smile, she buckled up. He pulled out of the parking lot and onto the road.

"You must think I'm cursed," she mumbled.

"And there I was thinking I was your bad luck charm." He gave her a sideways glance and smiled. "We'll find her."

She nodded and lifted her phone to dial her sister again. This time, the call beeped and went straight to her full voicemail box. "Wish she'd answer." She didn't like feeling like this, panic rising to burn the back of her throat.

"Tell me about her."

She dropped the phone to her lap and drew a deep breath. "Like I said, she's eighteen. She's smart. She graduated in the top ten percent of her class. We're waiting on letters from several colleges, but she hasn't been exactly running to the mail box. I was getting worried she didn't want to go. Now, I don't care if she wants to keep working at the Dollar Tree or not."

"This boy she's with...?"

"Brady. He's a nice kid. Cute. He's a cowboy, works on a ranch. He's...outdoorsy. It's why they're camping. She's never been."

"So, he won't get lost in the woods."

She knew what he was doing. Getting her to list reasons she shouldn't be afraid. "No, he's familiar with the area. His family goes out there to hunt and fish."

"That's good. He'll keep her safe."

"I hope so."

Cochise dropped his right hand from the steering wheel and captured hers. He gave it a squeeze then kept holding it as he drove. Gradually, she felt her panic lesson. She could breathe again. "Thanks," she whispered.

"Told you before. I have your back." He cleared his throat. "We'll take my vehicle."

She grunted. "Don't trust my truck?"

"No," he said, dragging out the word. "Your truck's great for one as old as it is. The engine's in good shape. But I have gear in the back of mine we might need."

She nodded. "I wasn't arguing."

"I wasn't dissing your wheels." He opened the hand that cupped hers.

Knowing he was offering to release her, if she

DELILAH DEVLIN

wanted him to, she threaded her fingers with his and give his hand a squeeze. Whether for comfort or because she liked him, she wasn't ready to decide why she wanted to accept his gesture. She just knew she needed the connection.

Cochise wasn't an easy man to get to know. But she knew that neither was she. Her glance went to the visor. He had secrets. Maybe she'd learn a few on this trip.

By the time they returned to the office, another vehicle was parked in front. Cochise eyed the banged-up red Jeep and figured it belonged to the new guy. Good. They'd need more boots on the ground.

He followed Sammy as she made her way inside. All the while, he couldn't help but smile a little. The woman who had a beef with bounty hunters was about to immerse herself in a hunt.

Everyone was gathered around Brian's desk.

Jamie was folding printouts of maps and handed one to Sammy. "Mark the place you think your sister and her boyfriend might be."

Sammy took a seat at an empty desk and pulled out her park map to compare.

Cochise turned to the new guy.

He stood beside Brian, leaning over his shoulder as they both read from the list of charges against Luke Ford. From the back, Cochise noted the guy was

42

ripped. He wore a navy MBH tee that hugged his torso, faded jeans, and combat boots. His hair was cut short and was a medium brown.

Cochise cleared his throat.

The new guy turned, his blue gaze sweeping over Cochise. "Hear you were a Ranger, too," he said. "I was in alpha company, third battalion."

"Third battalion, too. Charlie company." Cochise held out his hand, but then let it slowly drop when he realized the new guy didn't have one to shake.

"They call me Hook," he said, his eyes narrowing, but a hard smile beginning to stretch.

"Hope you weren't right-handed," Cochise muttered, holding out his left.

Hook held his gaze for a long moment then laughed as he shook Cochise's hand. "Yeah. Took some getting used to, but I can fire just fine with my left; just don't expect to be able to read my handwriting."

Cochise noted the sleek metal prosthetic, and that the cuff was below the elbow. Hook had been lucky. There were pockmarks and a few small burn scars disappearing under the arm of his tee. "IED?"

"Yeah. In southeast Afghanistan."

"I'm glad you're here," Cochise said, narrowing his gaze. Most amputees he knew didn't like to be coddled. Best to learn up-front whether Hook still had a sense of humor. "We've been short-*handed*."

Hook groaned, and then chuckled. "I guess you still are."

"Glad to see you two are bonding," Brian muttered wryly and shook his head.

"We ready?" Jamie called out. She glanced at Hook. "You'll ride with me and Sky. Hope you're not allergic to dogs, because Tessa's going, too." Her glance shot to Sammy. "You bring something we can use for scent, just in case we need it?"

Sammy nodded. "Cochise suggested it."

Jamie glanced around. "Well, let's roll. If we start now, we can be in Eureka by early afternoon."

Back in his truck, Cochise found he was relieved with the travel buddy assignment. Sammy was close by. He'd keep an eye on her. The possessive way he felt didn't have a thing to do with how she smelled—of strawberry shampoo and her own sweet musk. Or the fact her hair was beginning to curl, escaping its tight band. In casual clothing, as opposed to her uniform and underlying Kevlar, her chest was fuller than he'd thought. His groin began to tighten, so he eased back from wondering what she looked like nude, which was straight where his thoughts had gone back at her apartment when she'd walked out fresh from her shower. At that moment, he'd realized she was just about perfect. Perfect height to rest against him, her head on the edge of his shoulder. Perfect curves. In jeans, her ass appeared more rounded, making his fingers itch. Shit. He was doing it again.

He followed Sky's SUV out of town.

"So, you're from around here...?" he murmured,

just for something to say, because he didn't want any awkwardness between them during the drive, and she needed a distraction, so she wouldn't climb the walls.

"Libby, actually. Dad had a small mechanic's shop there. Sis and I moved here after they were gone."

"You said it was just you and your sister..."

She turned her head and glanced out the passenger-side window. "Yeah, Mom and Dad...they died together. Their car broke down in a blizzard. Kind of ironic, huh? Him being a mechanic. Guess he didn't know how high the snow had gotten. He turned on the engine to keep warm, and they both just...went to sleep."

"Sorry to hear that." From the corner of his eye, he watched her shake her head.

"That was nine years ago. The court gave me custody of Sheri when I proved I could support us both. Had to sell our house, though. The proceeds paid our rent for the first couple of years. Then I went to the police academy in Helena. Worked in Bozeman's PD for a few years. But I wanted to get closer to home, get out of the city. I saw the posting for the deputy's position in Bear Lodge and applied."

"It seems like a nice, quiet place to raise a kid."

"It has been." She raked a hand through her hair and tugged away the hairband. Her hair spilled around her shoulders. "What about you? What's your story? How about starting with your name?" She gave him a sideways glance. "Cochise is Apache. That would put you pretty far from home."

Cochise grimaced. "My mom was Blackfoot from Browning, but she joined the Army after high school and ended up in Fort Huachuca, Arizona, where she met my dad. He was mostly white with a drop of Apache. He didn't stick."

"And your mom?"

He sucked in a breath and let it out slowly.

"Sorry, didn't mean to pry."

Cochise shook his head. His hands tightened on the steering wheel. He'd been the one to initiate this conversation when he'd asked her personal questions, but he never talked about his past. He wondered if maybe it was because no one had ever dared to ask. "Guess you should know why I won't rest until your sister's found," he said, feeling like he was chewing on the words. "When I was overseas, first tour, there was a home invasion. My mom fought back, and the bastards killed her. They kept my sister alive for a little while." His jaw tightened as he glanced at Sammy. "Maria was eighteen and in her last year of high school."

He hadn't mentioned that to a soul in a long time.

Sammy's head lowered. "Sorry, Cochise."

"Yeah. Me, too."

Sammy cleared her throat. "That her picture clipped to your visor?"

He reached up, flipped down the visor, and slid the photo free.

When he handed it to her, she held it by the edges. "She was beautiful."

"It was her smile. Everyone noticed that first. It's what I miss most," he said, his voice gruff.

She handed him back the photograph, and he slid it under the clip and turned up the visor.

"We'll find your sister, Sammy. She's the first priority. Not the bounty."

"Thank you."

Her glance went to the side window again. "I've lived in Montana all my life. Must be really different from Arizona or Denver."

Glad for the change of topic, he nodded. "I like it. I don't plan to go anywhere." He wasn't sure why he said that last bit, but she turned her head and smiled. When he placed his hand on the console between them, she placed her hand atop his. With a slight turn, he captured it. Somehow, it felt natural. He blew out a breath and decided to cut to the chase. "I don't date."

"I don't either," she said, sounding a little breathless. "I have my sister. Having men around...that would just be awkward."

Tension stretched between them. He knew she was waiting for him to get to the point. He cleared his throat. "I eat." *Jesus, fuck.* Could he sound any more ridiculous? From the corner of his eye he watched her press her lips together. Was she trying to hide a smile?

"Um, so do I. Maybe when this is over, we could...eat together?"

He squeezed her hand. "I'd like that. You could bring her."

She laughed and waved a hand at her face. "It just got hot in here."

Cochise grinned and gave the road his attention. He didn't date women. When he got too edgy to stand his own company, he found a bed partner. But with Sammy, he thought he might like something... different. In quiet times, he barely tolerated his own company, but she was easy to be with, despite her sometimes-frosty disposition. Or maybe because of it.

The radio on the dash squawked. "Hey, Cochise. Over," came Jamie's voice.

He let go of Sammy's hand, reached for the radio, and depressed the talk switch. "Yeah, Cochise here, over."

"Jamie, here. I found a motel near the trailhead Sammy marked where we'll start our search. We'll need to contact the park service and local PD to let them know we'll be out there. Sky and I will check the Ford cabin on the way. I'll need you to interview park rangers to see if they remember seeing Sheri and her boyfriend. Over."

From the corner of his eye, he noted Sammy's nod. "Roger, anything else?"

"Two rooms or one? Queen beds. Over."

Cochise thought he heard an edge of laughter in her voice.

Sammy coughed. "One," she said in a small voice.

Cochise's blood quickened. "One, out." He shot her a glance. "You sure?"

"We're adults. I'd just as soon not be alone," she said the last in barely a whisper.

"Roomies, then."

Her nod was quick. Again, her glance slid away to the road.

For the rest of the trip, Cochise's mind was filled with images of Sammy—in a T-shirt with her long legs bared. Resting against his chest; his fingers tangling in her curly hair. The one image he shied away from was anything at all happening below the waist, because the pounding pulse in his groin already had him half-hard.

He'd be her best buddy. The shoulder she'd lean on. But after this was done, good intentions would fly. She'd invited him to share a room. It had to mean something.

CHAPTER 4

AFTER DRIVING through the outskirts of Eureka, Sammy guided Cochise to the park entrance where Sheri and Brady had most likely entered the forest. They questioned the guy at the booth and showed him Sheri's picture. He didn't recognize her, but he hadn't been on duty the day before. He gave them directions to a building where park maps were distributed and rangers familiar with the trails could give advice.

There, they met Farley Whitehead, a park guide, whose bronze skin and near-black hair also marked him as Native American. As he glanced down at the photo, he nodded. "I remember them. Real pretty girl. Goofy guy. They were here yesterday morning. They had a map, camping gear. Told him to watch out for bears." His dark brows drew together. "They in any trouble?"

Sammy shared a glance with Cochise. "You

might want to warn folks a felon might be hiding in the woods here."

Farley nodded and tapped his cellphone, which was in his front pocket. "Got a bulletin a little while ago. You talking about Luke Ford?"

They nodded.

"You with those bounty hunters who're tracking him?"

"Yeah," Cochise said, "and she's a sheriff's deputy," he said, nodding toward Sammy.

"There's gonna be all kind of law enforcement stomping around the woods, looking for him and advising hikers to leave," Farley said. "Be careful out there. Your sister should be easy to spot. She had a bright yellow backpack, kind of hurt my eyes. And if I see your sister, I'll tell her to sit tight someplace safe."

"Thank you," Sammy said, reaching out to shake his hand.

"Good luck."

When they left the building, Sammy shivered although the temperature was warm. "We know where they started. We need Tessa to track them."

"Have to see what Jamie and Sky turn up first. Let's head to the motel and dump some of our stuff."

"We need to hit an outfitter store, too. I need hiking gear."

Cochise nodded. "I have a backpack and a sleeping bag. You'll need the same. We also need tack, so we don't go hungry."

"Should have MREs for sale there, too." She pulled out her phone and located an outfitter's store with everything they needed. "Text Jamie," she said, "tell them where we're headed. Ask them if they need us to pick up anything."

"I'm sure Jamie has all her gear—Tessa's, too. Let's just worry about you."

They hit the store, purchasing a backpack, bedroll, rain poncho, a Camelbak water reservoir, and enough MREs to see them through a couple of days of hiking. At the motel, Sammy hung back while Cochise got the room key. She was having second thoughts about sharing a room with him. Did he think she wanted more than just his company? Did she want more than the comfort his presence gave her?

After he slid the key card into the lock, he shoved open the door and stood back to let her enter first. Ever the gentleman. And he was carrying her bag again.

He set it on one bed then dropped his bag on the other. "I'm gonna grab a quick shower."

Knowing he'd been up most of the previous night, she didn't begrudge him the time. She set the large bag with her purchases on the mattress, and then turned away as he drew clothing from his duffel. She didn't want to see his underwear. If she did, she'd imagine him in it for the rest of their time together.

After the bathroom door closed, she let out a deep breath and sat on the edge of the bed. The springs squeaked. Which made her giggle. Good Lord, now she imagined just how noisy it could get in the room.

Sammy shook her head. Why was she thinking about having sex with a guy she barely knew when her sister was out there, possibly in the path of a desperate criminal who got off on hurting women?

She moved to an armchair and sat. The sound of water running was the only noise in the room. For the first time in hours, her mind slowed. This was all too real. She could lose her sister.

Pulling her knees up under her chin, she prayed. "Please be safe, Sheri. I'm coming."

* * *

Cochise stood under the cool water for a long time, long enough his erection finally waned. After scrubbing up and shaving the scant whiskers on his chin, he rubbed a towel over his hair and dressed in boxers and jeans. When he pulled open the door, his gaze sought out Sammy, who sat on a chair, her eyes wet and widening as they trailed over his bare chest.

A twinge of pain tightened his chest, and he strode toward her. Kneeling beside her chair, he slowly pulled her into his arms and hugged her against his body. He didn't know what he was doing, but he followed his instincts.

She lowered her legs between them and leaned her chest against his, nuzzling into the corner of his neck. He liked the way she felt. So warm. Solid, with enough padding to please any man. He noted the way her soft breasts mashed against his pecs and wished there weren't any layers of fabric between them, not because he was ready to pounce on her, but because he wanted to hold her, skin to skin. There was comfort in that.

She moved closer, her thighs opening, and he pulled her off the chair and knelt with her on his lap as she locked her strong legs around his hips. For a long moment, they rested against each other, just breathing. Cochise felt the tension in her body ease.

But then her hips moved in a tiny, shallow grind.

His heartbeat thudded for several beats then quickened.

Her fingers gripped the corners of his shoulders. Without a word spoken between them, he rose and carried her to the bed.

When he went to one knee on the mattress, he pulled back his head to meet her gaze. "This what you want?" he asked, his voice going rough.

She nodded and leaned back to pull her tee over her head.

He unsnapped her bra in the back and helped her draw it off her arms. Then he glanced down, taking in the soft round breasts with their puckered, rose-brown nipples and leaned against her chest. His breath...her breath...left in a long, drawn-out sigh as they moved together.

When her gaze went to his mouth, he took his

cue, bending to capture her lips in a kiss that started tentatively but quickly ignited into passion. He scraped his fingers through her thick, curly hair and tilted back her head as he plunged inside her mouth, his tongue stroking hers. Her breasts shivered against him, and he drew back. "More?" he asked, knowing he had to ask, but hoping she wouldn't step on the brakes.

"Let me up," she whispered.

Before he had a chance to be disappointed, she stood and toed off her boots. Then she unbuttoned her jeans. Sitting on the edge of the bed, he took over, sliding his hands inside to cup her soft ass.

She gave a nervous laugh. "Let me get them off first."

From inside her jeans, he shoved them downward. He could feel his face hardening along with his cock, and he didn't want to scare her, but his need rode him with the first sight of her light-brown ruff. When she kicked away her jeans, he lifted his butt and scraped off his own clothing. He slipped a condom from his wallet, smoothed it down his shaft, then scooted backward on the bed, knowing where her gaze was locked.

She followed him, her breasts swaying beneath her as she crawled over him. She must have been feeling just as desperate as he was, because she didn't waste any time gripping his cock and positioning it between her folds. Then she slowly sank, taking him inside.

"Oh God," she whispered as she took him, not stopping until she rested against his groin. "We're really doing this," she said, her mouth twitching with a little bit of a smile.

"You are," he rasped. Then he cupped her breasts and rubbed his thumbs over the hard tips.

She bent over him, placing her hands on his chest. When she began to move, he let go of her to watch her tits bounce as her movements gained in speed.

He loved the wet heat of her. Loved her sighs and moans. But what she did next blew his mind.

She straightened, locked her gaze with his, and lifted her hand, holding it over her left breast. She slapped the underside, jiggling it. Then she thrust her chest forward in invitation.

He wasn't sure, didn't want to do the wrong thing, but he reached out and smacked one breast then the other, watching as her face screwed up in pleasure. Encouraged, he slapped her again then tweaked both tips, giving them hard twists. The slackening of her jaw confirmed this was what she needed. A little pain with the pleasure. So, he leaned up to suck one tight nipple between his teeth. He clamped his teeth around the tip and shook his head, growling a bit, because Jesus Christ he was almost at the edge.

Her fingers raked his scalp, her pussy clenched. Her hips moved in slow grinds, and then halted. "Please," she whispered.

Without any hesitation, he took over, pushing her off his cock and to her side, then coming up to guide her to her hands and knees. When he knelt behind her, he parted her buttocks and slid his cock between them in long teasing glides.

She didn't shy away, but her hands fisted in the sheets, and she turned her head to the side so that she watched him from the corner of her eye. There was a wariness, a fierce wildness in her expression.

Cochise raised a hand and swatted her ass.

"Again," she gasped.

He warmed her bottom with swats to both cheeks then clapped upward against her pussy, causing her to cry out.

Her torso quivered as she widened her knees and sank her chest to the bed.

Cochise thumbed her clit while he slowly pushed inside her pussy. His head fell back as he entered. She was so hot, so lushly wet. When he was balls-deep, he bent over her back and kissed her shoulder. "You surprised me, Sammy."

"I surprised myself," she said, her voice husky. "This isn't me. I don't know why..."

But he understood. Without the roughness, she'd feel guilty. "No worries, baby. I'll give you what you need."

She buried her face against her folded arms. "Just fuck me hard."

He planted his hands on the mattress on either side of her and hammered her, his motions hard, quick, and building friction as he pounded some more. The bed beneath them squeaked like a dog's chew toy, but the moist sounds they made, moving together, the slick slaps, only deepened his pleasure.

When her back curved upward, he stuck an arm beneath her breasts and hugged her against him, which shortened his strokes. He quickened his motions. "Touch your clit," he whispered in her ear.

"No, too much," she groaned.

"Now, baby, come with me."

She must have obeyed, because a moment later, she let out a reedy scream, and he let go, his balls exploding as come shot into the condom. He continued rocking against her until his body quaked. Halting, he drew her up, so that she sat, still impaled on his cock. With his hands, he stroked her breasts, her belly, her thighs, and then spread his fingers and tucked them along her stretched labia. "I want this again with you, Sammy McCallister."

Her breathing was harsh, her skin moist. "I've never... What I wanted..."

"Me neither, but I didn't mind. Sammy, I'll give you anything you need." He turned her cheek and leaned around to give her an openmouthed kiss.

A knock sounded on the door.

They both froze.

Locking his gaze with hers, he shouted, "Give us five." Then he lifted her from his lap and laid her on the bed on her side. He came down beside her, cupped her ass, and pulled her lower belly against his still-hard dick. "They won't say anything. No need to be embarrassed."

She gave him her signature scowl. "I won't jump their shit if they tease. And I'm not embarrassed." Her frown eased. "I needed that. I needed you."

Cupping her cheek, he scraped his thumb across her lower lip. "That wasn't just fucking, Sammy. Not for me."

Her lips tightened, but then one corner quirked upward. "Well, good." She wrinkled her nose. "I need to hit the shower."

He let her go, and she rolled off the bed and to her feet. As she walked away, he admired the bounce of her firm, round bottom. At the door, she glanced over her shoulder and caught him staring. "Not joining me?"

CHAPTER 5

TEN MINUTES LATER, they arrived at Jamie and Sky's room. The couple and Hook glanced up but quickly turned their attention back to the maps spread across one of the beds.

Relieved the rest of the team was ignoring the reason for their delay in joining them, Sammy moved to a chair beside them. But sitting only reminded her of what they'd done. A delicious ache throbbed between her legs.

When the knock had sounded on the door, her pussy had clenched around his cock, and instantly, she'd wanted more. He'd obliged her with a quickie in the shower, telling her afterward, "Now, you're clean inside and out."

Blushing at the memory of his sly words, she cleared her throat. "A park ranger recalled seeing them yesterday morning. And he got a bulletin about Ford. Was that you guys?"

Jamie nodded. "We stopped in and chatted with the PD. They called the park service then sent the warrant with his picture to circulate."

She drew a deep breath. "What's next?" This wasn't her rodeo. As anxious as she was to get out on the trails, she knew this team had more experience hunting criminals.

"His cabin was a bust," Jamie said. "Looked like he'd been there, though. He went through the garage, likely gathering gear. Could tell from the dust he disturbed."

"Wish we had his scent on something," Sky said, scratching between Tessa's ears. The dog's eyes were half-closed, and she leaned against his leg. "She's got a great nose."

Jamie nodded. "But our first priority is locating Sheri and her boyfriend—"

"Brady," Sammy said.

"Brady," Jamie said with a sharp nod. "As soon as they're safe, we'll switch gears and go after Ford."

Hook raked a hand through his short hair. "He may already be in Canada."

"It's hard to tell where the border is," Sky said, arching a brow. "No lines on the ground."

"Still don't want to run crossways with the Mounties," Jamie said, her tone dry.

Her fiancé shrugged. "They might turn a blind eye. I'm sure they don't want to deal with the guy."

"We're getting ahead of ourselves. So, the question is, do we head out now? Or wait until morning?" She glanced at Sky.

He pursed his lips then tipped his head. "I'd just as soon cover as much ground as we can before dark."

She cut to Hook.

He held up his hand. "I'm the newbie. I'll go with whatever the rest of you decide."

Cochise stared across at Sammy. "I say we leave now."

When Jamie met Sammy's gaze, the bounty hunter smiled. "Looks like we need to grab our gear."

"Thank you," Sammy said, relief flooding through her. She wouldn't rest easy until she knew her kid sister was safe.

"Be ready in..." Jamie glanced at her watch, "fifteen. Hope you have grub in your packs, because we aren't driving through any windows."

* * *

Taking advantage of the long early-summer day, they headed deep into the forest. Everyone wore holstered weapons and carried rucksacks filled with a change of clothing, MREs, and bedrolls tied to the bottoms of their packs. Hook carried the satellite phone case with his gear. Cochise and Jamie tucked GPS trackers into their back pockets. They didn't break to set up camp until well after eight PM. Although they didn't need to cook their food, Sky, Hook, and Cochise went deeper into the woods and gathered branches to make a fire to keep the critters away.

"I like her," Sky said, as he bent to pick up another branch to add to the stack he already carried.

Cochise didn't pretend he didn't know who his friend was talking about. "She's...prickly." And he smiled, thinking about the way her frown made him feel. It was its own sexy challenge.

"She doesn't appear to care much for our line of work..."

Cochise shrugged. "She works hard, by the book. I get it. She thinks we're a bunch of loose cannons, and that we don't care about rules."

"She must have been ready to shit a brick when Sky talked about crossing the border."

Sky shook his head. "Hopefully, we won't have to go that far." He squinted in Cochise's direction, wearing a half-smile. "Soooo..."

Cochise shook his head. "Not your business."

"I wasn't asking for the dirty details, it's just... kind of cool. Think she might be brought over to the dark side?"

"You mean, join the agency?" Cochise grunted. "Not a chance in hell. She already fished to see if the sheriff had offered me a job—which he did, by the way. I turned him down."

"Well, good. Back to the girl..."

Cochise gave him a glare, hoping it wasn't completely lost in the gathering darkness.

"Speaking from experience," Sky said, bending to

pick up another stick, "it helps that you have similar life experiences."

"Helps what?"

"Building a relationship."

Cochise's eyebrows shot upward. "Whoa, don't go marrying me off, just because *you're* heading into a noose. We just met."

"And you've already made the springs squeak."

Hook cleared his throat. "Kind of hard to miss that sound. It just kept building and building..."

Cochise couldn't help it, he laughed. "Enough. We're not talking about squeaks or whatever else happened between Sammy and me."

"Just..." Sky smiled. "Keep yourself open. The best things happen when you're ready for a change."

Cochise glanced into the dark forest canopy above them. "We better get back. The ladies can fend off anything on two legs, but I'm worried about the four-legged animals."

Sky gave a dirty chuckle. "Might need to keep your sleeping bag close to hers. Just in case."

"No squeaky springs out in the woods," Hook drawled.

"We're not... *Jesus.* Not within earshot." Cochise glared when both men's shoulders shook with laugher. "Fucking hell, you two. Do not embarrass her."

"All I'm sayin' is, she looked relaxed, man," Hook said, his wide grin gleaming in the near dark. "Maybe she needs a little stress relief."

"For fuck's sake, shut up."

The men were all laughing when they made it back to camp.

Jamie and Sammy glanced up, their eyebrows rising.

Cochise shook his head to forestall either woman asking what the guys found so damn funny.

While they'd been gone, the women had rolled out sleeping bags and placed the stones that had been gathered earlier around a pit they'd dug. An LED lantern lit the camp.

"About time," Jamie said. "I was just about ready to send Tessa out to find you."

"Ah, were you worried about me, babe?" Sky asked, wrapping an arm around her waist.

"I'll get the fire going," Hook said. "Got nothing better to do..."

Or anyone to greet. Cochise ignored everyone and bent over his backpack to extract an MRE. He held it to the light. "Ah, spaghetti. Why is it always spaghetti?"

Sammy chuckled and held up her meal pack. "I'll trade you. I have cheese tortellini."

He shot her a glare. "As long as I get the hot sauce, too."

She held out her bag.

He kept both and went to work using the chemical heaters to warm their meals.

When he handed her the spaghetti pouch, she

wrinkled her nose. "I could have followed the instructions."

"Why bother when I can do this in the dark?"

"Well, thank you." She slid her spoon into the pouch and took a bite. Then she tilted her head as she looked his way. "You know, Cochise, for someone who gives off a 'don't mess with me vibe', you're a gentleman." When he raised an eyebrow, she continued, "You're always opening doors, carrying my gear..."

His only response was a grunt. His mama had taught him manners. Around Sammy, he felt obliged to show them off. He sat cross-legged on his sleeping bag, tore open his pouch, then felt around inside the meal pack for the little bottle of hot sauce.

"This isn't bad," she said, digging her long spoon into her food, again.

Hook snorted from across the way. "Try eating these for months on end. You'll get to where you'd eat anything rather than face another of these things."

"Once, during one of my deployments, my team paid a villager for a chicken," Sky said, smiling. "Skinniest, rattiest thing you've ever seen. Well, my buddy had the job of preparing it for dinner, but when it got time to eat—there was no chicken roasting on any fire. The bird didn't know to be scared of him and followed him around like a damn puppy. The chicken became our tent mascot."

The men laughed, and Cochise glanced across at

Sammy. Her skin was golden in the firelight, her eyes luminous. She caught him staring and blushed.

"So, tomorrow," Jamie said, waving her spoon to get their attention. "Our map shows a split in the trail."

Sky swallowed down a bite and nodded his head. "Two trails. One that's more of a straight shot toward the border. The terrain's more rugged and leads into higher elevations. From the contour map, the other is the one a less experienced hiker would likely take—more even, and it follows a river."

"My sister's not an experienced hiker," Sammy said. "I doubt Brady would have taken her through the mountains."

"That hiking trail forks again into two long loops, one of which does get closer to the border."

Jamie's mouth pursed. "We'll split into two groups. Sky and I will take the shorter, more direct route. We'll have to hoof it. If Tessa doesn't find anything to track, we won't waste our time continuing to follow it. We'll double back and head your way."

Cochise glanced at Sammy. "You okay with that plan?"

She shrugged. "I'm not the hunter. I'm just along because I'd go nuts if I had to wait for word."

"It's your sister," he insisted.

Her head dipped. "I think she and Brady would have taken the second path. I'd just as soon follow it. Let Jamie and Sky have the mountain trail."

"Well, we'll have twilight just after five AM," Jamie said. "I plan to be packed and ready to head out before then."

There were nods all around, and they finished their meals in silence. When calls to nature had been completed, Cochise pulled out a small bottle of insect repellent. He squirted some on his palms then knelt beside Sammy. He rubbed it on her face and neck. "It's early in the season, but you don't want a bunch of mosquito bites."

"You know they're all staring," Sammy said, tilting her head toward the others. "You could have just handed me the bottle." Still, she held out first one arm, then the other, for him to slide on the lotion.

He grinned. "Where would be the fun in that?"

She shook her head, and then shivered.

"Get into your bag. You're cold."

"Yes, sir."

He waggled his eyebrows and leaned closer. "Save that for when we're alone," he whispered.

She winked and unzipped her bag. After removing her boots, she slid inside then bunched up the top of her bag to use as a pillow.

He stretched out on top of his, which he'd placed alongside hers.

Sighing, she rolled toward him. With the firelight behind her, he couldn't see her face.

Cochise reached out and trailed his fingers along her cheek. "Tomorrow, we'll find her." He felt her nod. Unable to stop himself, he slid his thumb over her lower lip.

Her breath caught. Then she turned her head and licked the length of his index finger. "I taste pepper sauce," she said. Then she sucked the tip into her mouth and bit into the pad of his finger.

He couldn't resist. He leaned toward her and kissed her, rubbed his lips against hers, then pushed his tongue inside her mouth. When he pulled back, he whispered, "If we were alone..."

She bit his lower lip. "If we were, I'd be more careful with my teeth..."

Cochise's cock stirred inside his jeans. He reached for her hand, moved it quietly to the front of his jeans, and cupped her palm against his growing erection. "I wouldn't mind a gentle bite or two."

She gave a very quiet groan and traced his length through the stiff fabric. "I'll expect reciprocation."

"Remember, I'm a gentleman. I'll do the honors first."

Her breath caught. "I'm not going to sleep a wink."

"If we wait until they fall asleep..."

Her breath gusted in silent laughter. "We'd never make it back into camp. Tessa would bark her head off."

"Do you really care?"

She leaned toward him and kissed his mouth. "No."

CHAPTER 6

SAMMY FELT LIKE A TEENAGER, slipping away in the darkness. She couldn't see a thing but held tight to Cochise's hand as he led her through the trees. She hadn't a clue how far they'd come, but she knew they'd have to keep quiet because sounds travelled in the night air.

When he came to a halt, she waited as he turned and began to pull away her clothing.

"You aren't just tossing it," she said, giving him her grumpy voice. "We'll have to find it all afterward."

"Can't you see the log on the ground?"

She peered around him and made out the long, low shape. "Convenient."

"I'm draping our clothes over it. One of us has to sit."

She choked back a laugh. "So, one of us is risking splinters?"

"That's what the clothes are for," he drawled.

She loved the husky note in his voice. "You naked yet?"

"Yeah."

She clutched his shoulders, careful to avoid the bite in the corner, and pushed him down on the log, which he allowed. Then she stepped between his open thighs. The second her breasts touched his chest, she moaned.

"Sweetheart, you have to be quieter than that," he whispered.

"I'll try."

His chest jerked in as he chuckled, and his hands found her waist and pulled her closer.

"I love how this feels," she said, rubbing against him. His skin was hot. And below, she felt the nudge of his cock against her belly. She dropped a hand to encircle his shaft and cupped his balls with the other. "Did I mention before how much I like *this*?" she said, giving him a stroke.

"No," he said, sounding a bit choked. "You never said..."

"My bad." Again, she rubbed her body against his, and then slowly dropped to her knees.

"I said I'd do the honors first."

"But I'm already here. Just hope that pepper sauce is long gone..." she teased, and then she stuck out her tongue and licked the underside of his cock from his balls to the tip. "You're long, hunter. And thick. More than I'll be able to take." She wrapped her hands around his base then bent over the head. She sucked the cap into her mouth and pulled, her cheeks hollowing. Then she dove downward, wetting his length before replacing her hands and starting a slow push-pull motion with a hint of twist as she bobbed her head over him.

His hands sifted through her hair, combing, and then pulling. "Sammy, stop..."

But she didn't want to. She felt ravenous...and powerful. She pulled back just far enough to use her teeth to gently chew his cap. His body shivered. His thighs gripped the sides of her body. She'd never felt sexier as she resumed sucking.

Soon, her jaws ached, and her throat felt a little sore. When she lifted her head, she was panting. "Did you think to bring a condom?" She prayed he had but was already making mental calculations about the safety of fucking "uncloaked."

His hand left her and returned. A foil packet scraped over the tip of her breast. She grabbed for it, tore it with her teeth, then smoothed latex down his length.

As soon as she finished, he thrust his hands under her arms and forced her to rise. Needing no other encouragement, she climbed over his spread legs and settled her knees on the fabric draping the log.

While he reached between them to slide his cock between her folds, she rested her forehead against his. "We're going to leave stains on our clothes that'll be hard to explain in the light of day."

"Your knees okay?" he rasped.

"The tree's hard," she said, licking his bottom lip. "You're harder."

His hands clapped over her ass then gripped her hard and pushed her down until her pussy consumed his cock.

"I like how you fill me," she whispered.

"Baby, I like how fucking sexy you are. Your cunt's hot—on fucking fire."

She smiled against his mouth. "That's a lot of fucking. And when you say it, I like that other word, too."

"Sorry. It slipped out."

She kissed him. "Say it, again."

"Cunt," he whispered next to her ear.

As a reward, she squeezed her inner muscles all around him and bounced on her knees.

His fingers dug into her ass and forced her to move faster. When she grew breathless, he heaved upward. She clasped her legs around his hips and held tight as he moved toward a tree and leaned her back against it. His arms cradled her as he began to fuck, his strokes hard and jarring. Her breaths gusted with each upward thrust.

Tension built, and she raked his hair, tugging away the band that held it. She gripped his hair and pulled his head forward. Their lips met as he continued to pound against her pussy. Then her core tightened. She jerked back her head, hitting the tree, but she didn't care. "I'm coming," she gritted out.

73

"I'm there. Now, baby, now," he growled and powered into her.

Pleasure exploded, and she raked her nails across his skin as wave after wave of ecstasy flowed through her.

His movements slowed, but he still held her against his body. He nuzzled the side of her face, and she turned to meet his kiss. As their tongues caressed, she fought to calm her heart and slow her breaths. She scooped her lips over his then pulled back. "Stay inside me. Just a minute more."

He leaned her against the tree and rocked his hips, giving her gentle, soothing rolls. "Think you'll sleep now?"

She laughed and hugged him. "I think we both will."

She lowered her legs, and he disengaged, moving back.

"I'll have to use the flashlight to find all our clothes," he muttered.

"Don't you dare! Do you even know how close to camp we are?"

"Not really. I was a little distracted."

Laughing softly, they searched for their clothes, passing items as they identified them. He produced a travel-sized packet of wet wipes, and she could have kissed him again as she cleaned up. "You planned this, didn't you?"

"A guy can always hope."

Dressed, he led her back to the camp. They

entered slowly. Sammy cringed over every snapping twig, but thankfully, Tessa didn't stir. When she was safely inside her sleeping bag, she heard a rustling sound from the opposite side of the fire.

"Thought I heard a bear bellowing."

It was Hook's sleepy voice.

"There was no bellowing," Cochise whispered.

A snicker sounded from Jamie's place near the fire. "You two had Tessa whining."

So much for keeping secrets with this team. Sammy groaned in mortification and pulled the edge of the sleeping bag over her head.

* * *

The next day's hike was grueling—even for the men who were accustomed to long marches while carrying an eighty-pound rucksack.

Cochise kept glancing behind him to make sure Sammy was keeping up with the quick pace Hook set. So far, she was soldiering on. Every time he looked her way, she gave him a tight smile. He hoped she didn't have blisters forming on her feet. From her scratching, he guessed she'd gotten a few bug bites last night in places she'd rather not mention. As for himself, the ache in the corner of his neck was his only complaint. His body hummed.

The events of last night played in his mind throughout the day. The woman was game for anything. Strong and sexy. His only regret was the darkness that had hidden the sight of the things she'd done to him. The next time she took him in her mouth, he'd make sure every light in his place was on. That thought made him smile, because he had no doubt that while she'd be more than willing, she'd blush the entire time.

Sammy wasn't like any other woman he'd ever known. She was mixture of gruff and surly—like this morning when he'd passed her his packet of wet wipes. She'd taken one and couldn't meet his gaze, busying herself with double-checking her efforts to pack away her things, muttering as she did so rather than raise her eyes. But she also displayed an endearing lack of feminine self-confidence. The woman had no clue just how pretty and sexy she really was. Just watching her brush her hair and efficiently scrape it back into a sleek French braid turned him on, because the angle of the small of her back thrust out of her lovely, generous tits.

Every hour he spent in her company, he felt more ensnared. And he didn't mind that the trap was quickly snapping shut. He was grateful to be caught. He just prayed everything ended well in the next few hours, or he feared she'd close him out.

He understood mind-numbing grief. He'd spent years in a rage-filled solitude, despite the efforts of his friends and commanders. Slowly, the people who'd cared about him had faded away. He hadn't known he was lonely until he'd been hired by Montana Bounty Hunters and joined their dysfunctional but still highly functioning group, and now he'd met a woman he thought he might like to get to know, with hopes of climbing out of his solitary life. But first, they had to find her sister and the man who threatened everything Sammy held dear.

An hour ago, they'd split from Jamie and Sky as the couple followed the direct, northern route. Now, Hook, Sammy, and Cochise hiked over a gentle rise.

When he reached the top of the hill, he glanced out over a burbling creek. The trail ahead was empty for as far as he could see. He slowed his steps, waiting for Sammy to catch up to him.

When she came up alongside him, he continued to walk, matching his steps to hers. "How're you holding up?" he asked, shooting her a sideways glance.

She wrinkled her nose. "Don't ask. If I say how I really feel, you might not hear the end of my complaints."

He smiled. "This is what we call a 'forced march' pace."

"So, not designed to accommodate wimps. I get it. And I appreciate the fact you guys are pushing ahead so we can reach Sheri and Brady. I'll keep up."

"All right. So, does it help you keep going by talking to me or watching the back of my boots?"

Again, she scrunched her nose. "The boots. I'd just as soon save my breath for scurrying after you two."

"Let me know if we need to slow down. We'll break soon anyway."

"I'll do that." She lifted her chin, pointing down the path. "Now, scoot. I don't want to think about everything that hurts. I'll follow the boots."

"Sure you're not just avoiding talking to me about last night?" he asked under his breath.

"Last night? Oh, I don't recall all that much," she said, narrowing her eyes. "I was asleep inside five seconds of closing my eyes. A bear could have nibbled on my toes, and I wouldn't have noticed." Her glare dared him to contradict her.

"Right." He gave her a wink and stretched his stride to move ahead of her. Again, he swept the area ahead of them. The banks of the stream were edged with vegetation. To the left was a thick, old-growth forest of cottonwood, aspen, and birch trees. A hundred places for a criminal to hide. He looked for movement, for signs any human had met with violence, but wasn't really expecting to find them. Ford had to be moving fast. Why would he slow himself down with hostages?

Ten minutes later, Hook paused in the middle of the trail and drew his weapon.

Cochise froze in place and glanced back to find Sammy hurrying toward him.

As a precaution, he pulled his weapon from his holster and edged toward a tree while he scanned the area to try to figure out what had caught Hook's attention.

Suddenly, Hook crouched, his gaze moving to the woods around them, but then he shot forward, running toward something only he could see in the distance.

Cochise patted the air to tell Sammy to sit tight, but she scowled and ran past him, her own weapon drawn. He followed, keeping his gaze scanning, searching, while he kept his breaths even to calm his racing heart.

"Dammit, Sammy," he said under his breath as she drew nearer to Hook.

Ahead, Hook halted and went to his knees beside a tree.

Cochise's stomach dropped. He saw a pair of scuffed hiking boots attached to jeans-clad legs. He raced after Sammy and caught her around the middle. He turned her and pushed her back. "Wait," he said, and gave her a hard stare. "Watch our backs."

"My sister—"

"Wears size eleven shoes?"

Her glance cut to the boots again, and she slowly shook her head. With her chest heaving, she moved to a tree for protection and showed she was willing to guard the trail.

Cochise moved toward Hook. As he came around him, his heart thudded. Blood covered the front of a Seahawks T-shirt and a pair of grubby hands. The young man's throat had been cut. A bandana had been tied over the slit. His chest was moving shallowly, a gentle, ragged rise and fall.

"He was lucky," Hook said, gazing up at Cochise. "Neither jugular nicked. Just his windpipe. The bandana's keeping blood from filling his lungs. I'm not going to touch the bandana. It's the only thing keeping him alive." Hook bent toward the young man. "Brady," he whispered.

Cochise drew a deep breath, praying they were wrong. He was the right age. *Please don't let this be Sheri's boyfriend.*

The young man's eyes slowly blinked opened, and he glanced wearily up at Cochise and Hook then struggled to straighten.

"Best not to move, buddy," Hook said, clamping a hand on his shoulder. "We're going to get you help. Don't try to speak."

"We do need to know a few things though," Cochise said, going to a knee. "Are you Brady? Don't move your head. Squeeze my hand if you are," he said, lifting the man's hand.

A squeeze confirmed his identity.

Cochise took a deep breath. "As far as you know, is Sheri alive?"

Another squeeze, *yes*.

"This happen a little while ago?"

Yes.

"He find you two this morning?"

Nothing.

"Last night?"

Yes.

"The man who did this—was he bald with a tattoo of a skull on his forearm?"

Yes.

"Were they still following the trail?"

Another squeeze, although weaker.

Cochise gently gripped his shoulder. "You did good, Brady. We'll find her. But you have to hang on."

Tears filled Brady's pale blue eyes.

Cochise rose and strode toward Sammy.

"It's Brady, isn't it?" she asked, her expression stricken.

"Yes, he's alive. And he's confirmed that Sheri's with Ford."

Her hand went to her mouth, and she took two backward steps. Her wide, panic-filled gaze met his, and then she pushed past and ran toward the men at the base of the tree. She went to her knees beside Brady and Hook.

When Cochise reached them, she was leaning over Brady. "Sweetheart, you hold on," she said. "Hook's g-going to get you help. M-my f-friend and I are going after Sheri. We'll get her back, Brady."

Hook pushed up from the ground and took off his rucksack. Opening the top, he reached inside for the sat phone case and moved to the middle of the trail.

As he called for help, Cochise knelt beside the young man whose face was a chalky white. "Brady, you have to stay awake. Stay sitting, just like you are," he said, knowing Brady needed them to keep him engaged.

He'd been here so many times, holding a hand, touching a cheek, trying to keep an injured man in the "now" so he didn't slip away. "You were damn smart, kid. That bandana, sitting upright. You kept it together."

Brady's eyelids fluttered. The corner of his mouth twitched.

Hook returned. "I'll stay with him until help arrives. PD and park service are heading this way."

A sound in the distance drew their attention skyward. A helicopter was overhead, although they couldn't see it through the trees. More eyes on the ground. Cochise glanced at Sammy.

"Let's go," she said, and then without waiting for his response, she took off at a fast clip down the trail.

"Good luck," Cochise said to Hook. He bent and patted Brady's shoulder again, then he ran behind Sammy, knowing what she had to be feeling. He hoped like hell they found them before dark, because he worried about what Ford might do to Sheri without Brady as a buffer. His own sister's rape and murder were a horror he didn't want Sammy to suffer through. If he got the chance, he'd take the damn shot. No matter the cost.

CHAPTER 7

SAMMY SLOWED TO A JOG, knowing she had to go the distance. Brady's blood was still fresh. He couldn't have been there long. Her sister was near. She could feel it. Sammy was determined to find her.

With her head down, her pack snug against her back, she couldn't allow the strain on her muscles, on her heart, to slow her down. Her sister needed her.

Something glinted on the ground, and she slowed then stopped. A pale blue cord with a silver feather charm—one of the knotted bracelets her sister wore in a stack. She bent and snagged it from the ground, and then raised it high to show Cochise.

She checked the side of the trail, looking for any sign they'd entered the woods, but found nothing. So, she moved forward again, this time at a fast walk, following the trail, checking the sides, hoping she was right and that her sister was leaving breadcrumbs for rescuers to follow.

Maybe a quarter mile down the trail, Cochise called out. Her gaze followed to where he pointed.

A pale peach bracelet decorated with silver beads lay a foot from the trail.

She plucked it from the ground and touched it against her cheek. "That a girl, Sheri," she whispered. Hope swelled inside her chest. Her sister was keeping it together.

They searched the woods near where the bracelet had been dropped.

Cochise bent and brushed away leaves. A depression the shape of a booted heel was there on the ground. He glanced toward the forest and moved on, tipping a broken branch. The splintered edges looked fresh. "I think they've left the trail."

"Dammit, it's going to be harder to track them," she said softly.

He pulled a compass he wore on a beaded chain from around his neck. Holding it on his flattened palm, he turned. "The bracelet was there," he said, pointing behind her. "The broken branch..." He turned his body to follow the line both points made. "They're heading north now."

She drew her map from her back pocket and laid it on the ground. They knelt.

"This bend in the trail. That ravine..." He pointed at the map. "This is where we are." He used the side of his compass to measure the distance from their location to the border. His glance met hers. "They could be there by nightfall."

They heard sounds behind them. Rustling, stomping. Her breath caught.

"Has to be more of the search party," Cochise said, his hand closing around her forearm.

Although she hated turning back, they returned to the trail.

From the forest on the opposite side of the path, Sammy spotted a golden coat, a flash of a long, raised tail. Tessa burst into the clearing.

Relief flooded Sammy, and she fell to her knees to greet Tessa, who ran up to her and began licking her chin.

Sky and Jamie ran after Tessa. "We were with park rangers when they got the call from Hook. We followed your GPS tracker and went cross-country to find you."

Cochise wasted no time. "Sheri's been leaving us a trail."

Sammy opened her hand to show the two bracelets she held clenched in her fist. "She's been dropping these." She turned to point to the place where Ford and Sheri left the trail. "We think they're cutting through the forest to head straight to the border. Ford might have heard that helicopter and decided the trail was too out in the open." She dropped her rucksack from her back and rooted for the baggy with Sheri's T-shirt. As she handed the bag to Jamie, she said, "I can't tell you how relieved I am that you're both here."

That they'd arrived at this precise moment gave

her even more hope. Someone above was looking out for Sheri. Although Sammy had never considered herself a religious person, she couldn't argue with the fortuitous gifts they'd been given.

Jamie glanced at Cochise and Sammy. "Once Tessa begins tracking, she's going to move fast. We might want to dump our gear, so we can keep up."

After shoving ammunition into their pockets, they hid their rucksacks behind a tree.

Jamie handed out earpieces. "When we get close, we won't want to shout to each other." Then she took the baggie, opened it, and held it beneath Tessa's nose.

The dog buried her nose in Sheri's shirt. Her paws pranced, and her tail wagged.

Jamie laughed softly. "You love this part, don't you, Tess? Take a good sniff, baby girl." When she pulled the bag away, she gripped Tessa's collar and walked her to the place Sammy had indicated where Ford and Sheri might have left the trail. She bent over Tessa and gave the German command, "*Such!*" When she released the dog's collar, Tessa darted forward, her nose on the ground.

She sniffed left then right, and then must have found something that excited her, because she gave a growly whine and darted forward.

Sammy flew behind Jamie and Tessa, feeling as though she'd found her second wind. They moved quickly, down into a ravine and then up the other side, Tessa stopping here and there to find the trail then rushing forward again, her tail wagging.

Sammy nearly ran into Jamie when she suddenly halted. Breath hitching, Sammy moved to her side and glanced downward. Tessa was whining as she danced around a sunflower-yellow backpack. Red was smeared on the side of the bag.

Cochise cupped Sammy's hand. She leaned against his shoulder, taking strength from him. "It's her bag."

"I know."

"We have to be close."

Jamie knelt and touched the blood. "It's dry. Not fresh. Might be from the boyfriend," she said, glancing up at Sammy. Then she opened the baggie she'd carried into the forest and held it under the dog's nose again. "*Such!*"

Again, Tessa sniffed in a pattern, left to right, before moving to a new spot. The second she caught the scent, her tail wagged, and she shot forward again.

Ten minutes later, they followed a path that hugged an eight-feet tall rock outcropping, while the other side fell away into a deep, saddle-shaped depression.

Tessa found a pale green bracelet with a pineapple charm.

Jamie handed it to Sammy. "I like your sister. She's keeping a cool head."

Sammy took the bracelet and stuffed it into her front jeans pocket with the rest of them. Sheri would want them back. She'd been collecting them for months.

Up ahead, Tessa lifted her nose. Her body went completely still, and her ears pricked forward as she glanced down into the depression.

Jamie walked to the dog, knelt beside her, and clipped a lead to her collar.

They all crouched and held still, listening, hoping to hear what had alerted the dog.

Then Sammy heard it. Low cursing. A female crying.

"Fucking bitch!"

The sound came from directly beneath them.

"Looks like they fell," Sky whispered and pointed toward brush on the side of the hill that appeared flattened.

"Comms on," Jamie said.

Sammy reached to her earpiece and tapped it on.

"We'll need to come at them from both sides." Cochise glanced toward Jamie and Sky. "Why don't you two head farther down the trail and find a place to climb down. Sammy and I will head back about twenty. I saw rocks we can scale."

Everyone moved quietly apart. Sammy kept on Cochise's heels, following his example and crouching low in case anyone below happened to look up.

The rocks that lined a small gully provided a ladder for them to climb down into the depression. Once on the ground, Sammy again followed Cochise, moving tree to bush, taking cover as they grew nearer to the place where they'd heard the voices.

The fact Ford had gone silent alarmed Sammy. Had she come this far to lose her sister in the last few minutes? Then Cochise knelt behind a large leafy bush and motioned for her to join him. He pushed aside branches, giving her a view into a clearing.

Sammy gasped. Her sister was on her hands and knees, warily watching Ford as he paced beneath the bluff, his left arm held tight against his side as he studied the rocks.

After reassuring herself that her sister appeared fine, she studied Ford, noting the holster strapped to his thigh and the compass he held on his palm. They were maybe thirty feet away. Her sister knelt between them and Ford. From this angle, they couldn't risk a shot.

"We have eyes on Ford and Sheri," Cochise whispered. "He's armed. Might have injured his left arm."

"Almost there," Jamie said softly through the earpiece. "Left Tess in a down-stay on the trail above."

"Ford's thirty feet from us, but Sheri's between us."

After a couple of minutes... "We're at to your ten o'clock."

"I'm going to try to get Sheri's attention," Sammy whispered. "Tell her to keep down."

Cochise gripped her arm as she began to move

past him. His jaw tightened, and his gaze bored into hers.

I know, she mouthed, and then gave him a small, sweet smile. He was worried about her, which she appreciated, but she was a professional, too. She wasn't going to sit on her hands while the others put themselves in harm's way for her sister.

After a moment, his gaze fell away, and he released her and turned his attention back to the pair in the clearing.

Sammy felt warmed by his concern, and happy that he trusted her to do her part. He didn't like that he couldn't protect her, which was his instinct. Given his history, she understood.

She moved away, staying low, crawling on her belly at one point to sneak behind a bush about fifteen feet from her sister. There, she came to her knees and searched the ground for a pebble.

When she found one, she waited until Ford's back was to her and tossed the pebble at her sister, striking her arm.

Sheri glanced at her arm, saw the pebble on the ground, then frowned as she glanced toward the bush where Sammy sat hidden. Sammy pulled back a branch and placed her finger to her mouth.

Her sister's eyes widened then filled with tears. Sammy shook her head and let the branch conceal her again. As much as she wished she could have reassured her more, at least her sister knew she wasn't alone.

* * *

"Sheri knows we're here," Sammy whispered over the comms.

Cochise let out a breath. "Now, Sammy, sit tight."

"Ready when you are," she said, her tone even.

Stubborn woman. He was too worried about her, which he knew meant his brain wasn't where it needed to be. Again, he drew slow, calming breaths and attempted to clear his mind of any emotion. "You call it, Jamie, Sky."

"If we rush him, he'll have time to draw," Sky said.

"Anyone with a clear shot?" Jamie asked.

Silence.

"Okay, so we have to get closer," she said.

Cochise's heart settled. He leaned to the side to check Ford's location, estimating how close he would have to get, and at what angle, to take him down. "Sammy, sit tight. I'm getting closer. When we move, you look after your sister."

"Will do."

Cochise moved away from where he knew Sammy hid, not wanting to accidently draw attention her way. He made a wide circle, then moved with his back to the rocks at the base of the short cliffside where Ford and Sheri had fallen. With his weapon held up against his chest, he moved slowly, keeping his gaze to his right, knowing that he and Ford would eventually meet.

He was close enough he heard the man's feet stomping, and then the sounds stopped.

Cochise edged closer and peered around a rock.

Ford tossed a map to the ground beside Sheri, who angled her body away. When he went to his knees, he turned suddenly, snaked out an arm, and caught her wrist with his right hand. "This is your fucking fault. Think you could push me over the cliff, and that I wouldn't take you with me?" He pulled her so close his head was only inches from hers. "Stupid bitch, I coulda been in Canada by now."

Sheri's chin tilted upward. "Think the Mounties wouldn't know you're coming? People are out here, looking for you."

Cochise knew she was deliberately distracting him, but he needed Ford to move away. *Don't provoke him, girl.* He didn't want to see her get hurt.

With his face in profile, he saw Ford's lips pull away from his teeth in a snarl. "Maybe, but I still got you. Now that your boyfriend's not around to make noise..." He leaned toward her, and Sheri turned away her face. He gave her cheek a long lick.

Rage flared inside Cochise's chest.

"We have to hold steady," Jamie whispered. "He's too close to her."

Cochise drew deep breaths, again seeking that icy chill he always found, but this time, his body continued to vibrate. He pressed his back against the rocks, grinding against a rough edge to distract him from the urge to charge into the clearing.

About then, he heard a rustling near Sammy's position. He turned his head, knowing what was about to happen and unable to do a damn thing about it.

A moment later, Sammy walked into the clearing, her hands raised.

"Goddammit," Sky whispered. "What the fuck is she doing?"

Cochise watched in horror as Ford pushed off the ground and pulled his weapon, holding it out shoulder level and glancing around wildly, likely wondering if more people were in the bushes.

"It's just me," Sammy said.

Ford's eyes were wide and glaring. "Get over here," he said, jerking his gun to motion her forward. When she was just a few feet from him, he moved closer and pressed the muzzle of his pistol against her chest, right over her heart. "Who the fuck are you?"

Sheri began to sob, the sounds breathy and chopping apart.

Even though he was going nuts inside, Cochise couldn't help but admire Sammy's stillness.

"I was worried about my sister," she said, her voice low and calm. "She and her boyfriend showed me the trail they'd be following before they left home, so when they didn't check in with me last night... I had to come. I followed the trail, and then I heard you shouting. It's how I found you."

Ford moved the muzzle to her forehead.

Cochise's heart slowed. Cool prickled over his skin.

Sammy's shoulders stiffened. "Pull that trigger," she said, her voice dead calm, "and every cop and park ranger will be all over you. They know you're here. Brady was found. And he's alive."

Sheri cried out and covered her face with her hands.

Ford lowered his handgun and pointed it at her sister. "Get over there."

Sammy gave a curt nod and moved sideways to her sister.

"On your knees."

"Why are you wasting your time?" Sammy asked. "The border's just a few miles north. You don't need us slowing you down. Leave us. By the time we find any law enforcement, you'll already be in Canada."

"And if they find me first?" he snarled.

"You think a hostage is going to make a difference? You're only going to make it harder on yourself. We'll slow you down."

Cochise could tell her words were giving Ford second thoughts about his course of action. His gaze darted between the women and the woods.

When he glanced away, Sammy edged closer to her sister, and Cochise realized she was moving between Ford and Sheri. She'd set up his shot.

"Babe," he whispered, knowing she could hear him, "on your say, I'm ready."

"On three," she whispered.

Ford's gaze swung back, and he frowned. "What?"

"One, two...three!"

At the same moment she dove over her sister, Ford pointed his weapon at her back. Cochise didn't hesitate. He stepped away from the cliffside and fired, hitting Ford in the center of his chest.

Ford jerked and glanced down as blood blossomed and spread across his shirt. Confusion deepened his frown until his jaw slackened, and he fell first to his knees, and then toppled face-first into the dirt.

Cochise ran into the clearing, his heart racing, because he wasn't sure Ford hadn't fired.

He kicked away Ford's weapon, although he was certain the man was dead, then slid to his knees beside Sammy and her sister.

When he touched her shoulder, she glanced back and sagged against Sheri.

Cochise went with his gut and gathered up both women in his arms and held them against his chest. Both women were safe. Sammy hadn't been hit. He let out a shuddering breath.

Sheri pulled back first. "Brady's really alive?"

"Far as I know," Cochise said. "We left him with one of our team. Help was on the way. He was able to give us enough information for us to keep tracking you. His first thoughts when we found him were about you."

Her face crumpled, and she sank against his

chest. "That asshole cut his throat. No warning at all. We were doing everything he told us to do, and he still..."

Sammy reached out and cupped the corner of her shoulder. "Did he hurt you, Sheri?" she asked softly.

Sheri shook her head. "He walked into our camp last night, pointing that gun. Said we'd be taking a long walk with him. The way he looked at me..." Her mouth trembled. "Brady said we'd slow him down if he touched me. Made him pretty mad. This morning, he said he didn't need both of us. He stepped behind Brady and cut his throat. Then took his backpack and forced me to leave him. Hardest thing I've ever had to do. I was so sure he was dead." She sobbed against Cochise's chest.

Sammy's arm came around his back, and she leaned her weight against him. "You're probably pretty mad at me," she murmured.

Cochise closed his eyes, thinking about the moment she'd stood and walked toward Ford. "Pretty damn mad, yeah."

"I had to do it. We couldn't get close enough. If he'd heard us moving in... He was too close to her."

Cochise hugged her and kissed her forehead. "I get why you did it, but you owe me for scaring years off my hide."

A shrill whistle sounded, and barking sounded in the distance.

Already in the clearing, Jamie knelt beside them. She smiled downward. "Nice to meet you, Sheri

McCallister." She held out her hand, and Sheri shook it. "Nice trick with the bracelets."

Sheri wiped her eyes and gave a tremulous smile. "It's all I could think of." Her gaze went to Sammy. "I wasn't sure you'd even realize I was in trouble until it was too late, but I knew I had to try to send you a message."

"We're going to have to walk out," Cochise said. "You up for that? Were you hurt when you two went over the cliff?"

She gave him a crooked grin. "He broke my fall." Her smile faded. "He's dead, right? I know I shouldn't wish it—"

Cochise cut her off with a shake of his head. He didn't want her feeling even an ounce of regret over Ford's death. "Yeah, he's gone. He won't hurt anyone ever again."

* * *

They left Sky and Jamie with the body and trekked back in the direction they'd left Brady and Hook. Along the way, they retrieved all the backpacks. As Cochise shouldered three bags, they heard the *whomp-whomp* of helicopters flying above them. About midway back, they met up with park rangers, and they radioed to federal authorities who'd arrived to assist with the search.

After giving them directions to Ford's body, and promising they'd speak with authorities to give their statements before leaving the park, they continued along the trail. When they reached the path, they found Hook sitting with Farley Whitehead, both of them eating MREs when they arrived.

Sammy glanced around but saw that Brady was no longer there.

"Where's Brady?" Sheri asked, wringing her hands.

Farley gave her a smile. "Your man was airlifted a little while ago." He held up a radio. "They already have him at the hospital in Kalispell. Looks like he's going to make it."

Sheri closed her eyes. "Thank you, Jesus."

Cochise moved toward Farley and shook his hand. "You got out here pretty quick."

Farley pointed down the trail. A horse was tied to a tree, eating leaves from a bush. "You folks sit tight. We've got people coming on ATVs to get you out."

Sammy's shoulders sagged. They wouldn't have to make another "forced march" to get back. Thank God. Now that the danger was past, fatigue was hitting her hard.

Cochise dropped the backpacks and began pulling out MRE packages. He quickly heated meals for the women and himself. Sheri tried to wave away the one he handed to her, but he kept it outstretched. "You're running on fumes. When the adrenaline begins to leave your system, you're going to need this. Eat. Quit being stubborn."

Sheri gave him a little frown but begrudgingly

accepted the meal, and then sat cross-legged on the trail and began to eat.

"Stubborn must be in the genes," Cochise drawled.

Sammy arched a brow. "And you're not?"

He grunted and dug into his food.

Hook chuckled.

Sheri glanced at Sammy. "You know these guys?"

"They're...friends," she said. "Bounty hunters from Bear Lodge. They helped me track you down."

"So, they were getting paid to bring Ford back? Does it matter that he's dead?"

Hook shrugged. "We'll get our bounty."

"Good." She was silent for a moment, and then said, "So, how does one become a bounty hunter?"

Sammy choked on her food and began coughing.

Cochise grinned. "Most of us at Montana Bounty Hunters are ex-military, but a law enforcement background comes in handy, too. One of our hunters was just plain nosy enough to be really good at tracking people. There's not any *one* way to become a hunter."

Her sister studied his face. Sammy knew she should be a little alarmed at her interest. She didn't want Sheri sidetracked by becoming enthralled with her rescuers.

"My sister wants me to go to college. I might look into Criminal Justice."

"You could be a lawyer..." Sammy muttered.

"Where would be the fun in that?"

Hook and Cochise laughed—no doubt because

Sammy knew she must look poleaxed. She schooled her expression into a neutral mask and finished her meal.

Just as they were packing away their trash, the sound of engines could be heard in the distance. Four ATVs appeared over a hill and slowed to a stop.

Farley strode toward the group and chatted with them while the rest of their party hung back. Sammy wanted all of them to get out of the woods together, but if the rangers couldn't accommodate them all, she knew the men would insist on her and her sister leaving.

As it turned out, that was exactly what happened.

Sammy felt a flutter of panic as the women were herded toward the vehicles. There was no time for her to have a word alone with Cochise, to thank him. And to find out when she might see him again.

No time to kiss him goodbye—however awkward that might feel with an audience.

After she climbed on behind a park ranger, she glanced over her shoulder. Cochise's steady gaze locked with hers for a long, charged moment, and then the engine started, and they pulled away.

Sammy consoled herself knowing that she and her sister would be delayed while they gave their statements before they'd be released. Surely, she'd see Cochise again. After all, she and her sister would need a ride back to Bear Lodge.

CHAPTER 8

A WEEK PASSED. A week that was so busy Sammy had little time to worry over the fact Cochise hadn't contacted her. *As if.*

The day they'd left the Kootenai forest, she and Sheri were met in Eureka by Sheriff Miller. He wore a huge smile on his face when the ATVs pulled up outside the park building, where authorities had set up an ad hoc operations center. The number of people who'd poured into Eureka to assist with the search was shocking to Sammy, given that no one had known for sure that a hostage situation was occurring until Hook had called in asking for assistance to airlift Brady out of the woods.

All Sammy could think was that Jamie had gone straight to worst-case-scenario territory when she'd contacted the PD and park service, and then the authorities had reacted with an overabundance of caution.

The sheriff greased the wheels, getting them interviewed the second they entered the building, and then hustling them into his SUV to return them to Bear Lodge. Sammy couldn't very well complain about the haste of their departure. Sheri was near the end of her rope worrying over Brady.

The trip back had felt surreal. Sheriff Miller wanted the details of the search and takedown and nodded when she described Ford's final moments.

After she'd finished with her story, he sighed. "Mercier would make a great deputy. Any chance you can convince him?"

She chuckled. "After seeing him work with his team, I know he wouldn't want the job."

"Do I have to worry about you jumping ship?" he asked, shooting her a worried glance.

"Oh, hell no."

"That's good," he said, his voice gruff. "You work well with other agencies. Would you consider working investigations?"

Her eyebrows shot upward. "I'd love to."

When the sheriff dropped them at Sammy's truck, she'd asked Sheri for moment as she ducked inside the bounty hunters' office to see Brian Cobb. She'd used the excuse of returning the earpiece she'd forgotten she was wearing, and then asked him to confer her thanks for everything they'd done to help rescue her sister.

Brian's eyes had twinkled as she'd stalled a second longer than she should have, trying to figure out how to leave a message for Cochise. He'd cleared his throat and asked her for her cellphone number—in case they needed to reach out to her for anything. Grateful he hadn't teased her, she scribbled her number on a pad and waved goodbye.

After a quick shower and change of clothes, the women had headed to Kalispell where they'd remained for the next two days, waiting to see Brady every time he woke up and the nurses allowed him visitors. His family had all given her big hugs and thanked her for her efforts to save their "boy."

Sammy had shaken her head. "He saved himself and my sister. If he hadn't thought quickly..."

Brady's father had puffed up. His eyes misted. "That's my boy."

The family had welcomed the women to the corner of the waiting room they'd claimed for their family, sharing food other relatives brought in throughout the day.

After Brady was moved from the ICU, the women made another trip home for Sheri to pack a bag and head back to spend time with Brady. His family didn't mind the intrusion, not when Brady's face lit up like a Christmas tree every time she entered his room. Sammy arranged for Sheri to stay in the same hotel as the Brady family, and then watched as her sister drove off in her own car. The next few days that Sammy spent alone was the longest period she'd ever spent alone in their home.

Which gave her plenty of time to mull over her future and her feelings for Cochise.

Although she'd only known him for a short while, she was pretty sure she loved him.

When that had happened, she wasn't sure. But she suspected the moment might have been on that first morning, when he'd looked across the bench seat of her vehicle and told her, *Whatever move you want to make...*

She recognized and understood his need to protect women, all women, from harm. It was ingrained. Earned through his deep grief. And yet, he'd proven his respect for her skill and strength on that first day when he'd offered her the lead.

After more days passed, Sammy began to worry that he simply didn't feel the same way she did about him. He didn't call. Not once.

Back at work, she set her mind to her job, kept tabs with a very happy Sheri, and muddled through her days. Her nights, however, were interminable as she relived the fleeting moments she'd spent inside Cochise's arms. She'd never experienced that kind of passion before and knew her life would be pretty empty if she never had that again.

* * *

Cochise was happy he was stuck on a hilltop in the middle of fucking nowhere, sighting down his rifle at a blue pup tent.

He was happy because, for once, he was alone. Just the mosquito buzzing next to his ear for company. Since he'd left Eureka, he'd been surrounded with people who didn't get why he was fucking irritated as hell that this hunt wasn't already over.

The first night, after he'd spent the afternoon on horseback heading into high country near Whitefish, he'd muttered and bitched at Reaper and Dagger because they hadn't already found Maynard Wallace.

"He's a slippery bastard," Reaper drawled.

His wife Carly openly stared at Cochise, and he knew she was wondering what bug had crawled up his ass.

"He's pissed because he didn't say 'no' when I asked him to come up here to finish this," Jamie drawled.

"Why's that?" Carly asked, not looking away from him.

Cochise aimed a glare at Jamie, but that didn't shut her up.

"He's pissed because he didn't get to kiss a certain deputy goodbye."

"Oh?" Carly's eyebrows shot up. And then a smile stretched. "You wouldn't be talking about that cute Deputy McCallister back in Bear Lodge, would you?"

When Cochise's glance went skyward as he counted slowly in his head, she whooped.

"All right, I have to hear everything," she said,

gripping Jamie's arm and tugging her away from Sunny Holcomb's barn, where wranglers were saddling extra horses the hunters had rented for the trek into the mountains.

And, of course, Jamie had shared every embarrassing detail, including sound effects to imitate squeaking bedsprings and bear-like bellows. As if he and Sammy had actually made that much noise. He'd never known Jamie was such a damn gossip.

The guys had ribbed him endlessly. Hook had offered him the use of the sat phone to give Sammy a call, but Cochise didn't want an awkward as hell call. He wanted Sammy resting against his body when he told her how much he'd missed her and wanted a chance for them to make things work.

But as the days stretched into a week, he knew he'd made a mistake not accepting that offer of a call. Especially after the sat phone got stomped on by a horse, ending any chance of him letting her know he hadn't forgotten about her. That he was doing his best to finish this damn job, so he could spend time with her.

"I hear movement below the ridge," came Hook's voice. He was parked on a ledge below where Wallace had pitched his tent.

When Tessa had led them to the empty tent, they'd figured Wallace was away hunting. From the depth of debris in the firepit, Wallace had been here a while, trying to "live off the land" rather than show his face in public. They'd been sitting on the campsite since yesterday, dug in and camouflaged, waiting for him to return.

They had three days left to find him and bring him in before the $15,000 bond expired. To Cochise's mind, split so many ways, the bounty wasn't worth his being stuck in the mountains.

Hook drew a breath and released it before looking down his scope again.

A head appeared over the rim of the ridge. Wallace hauled himself up, his rifle slung over one shoulder, and dropped a string of dead birds on the ground beside the fire pit.

The embezzler had lost a few pounds. His flannel shirt hung on his shoulders. A steady diet of protein could do that to a man. He'd probably thank them if they offered him a candy bar.

From the corner of his eye, he watched as Sky rose into a crouched position. "Maynard Wallace!" he shouted. "Fugitive Recovery Agents! We have you surrounded."

Wallace glanced at the birds then dove for the dirt beside his tent.

"Seriously, asshole?" Sky said. "We have you surrounded. You're not going anywhere." Sky tapped his ear. "Cochise, you want to show him we're serious?" he said softly.

Cochise scanned the camp through his scope and noted the Billings Bulls hockey pennant fluttering on the center tent pole. After regulating his breathing, he gently squeezed the trigger.

The shot rang out, severing the pennant from the pole and sending it fluttering to the ground.

"Goddammit, don't shoot!" Wallace said. He went to his knees and held up his hands.

"Really, that's it?" Reaper sounded disappointed.

"He's terrific at hiding," Carly said dryly. "Doesn't mean he's brave."

"While you're on your knees, move to your right, away from your weapon," Sky called out.

Still cussing, Wallace sidestepped on his knees.

"I need you to remove your shirt, buddy," Sky said, continuing issue orders. "We have to know you don't have any other weapons on you. Move slowly."

Cochise watched his every move and twitch, his finger a quarter inch from the trigger.

When Wallace bared his pearl-white chest and rotund belly, a snicker sounded. "I can't ever *un*see that," Lacey said.

"Hook, can you move in?"

Hook rose with his Glock in hand and moved purposefully toward Wallace, his gaze never leaving the kneeling man. When he stood behind him, he said, "Go to your hands and knees. Now, lie flat and lift your hands behind your head." After Wallace complied, Hook knelt with a knee in the center of Wallace's back, holstered his weapon, then quickly cuffed him, using just one hand. When he rose, he dragged Wallace to his feet. "All clear," Hook called out.

The team moved in. Sky snagged the rifle then

searched the tent, backing out with two more weapons in his hands. Then he dragged out a backpack and emptied the contents on the ground. He emptied the chambers of the guns and set them beside the pack.

"I'll gather his belongings," Lacey said. As she repacked his things and wrapped the weapons in T-shirts, Dagger took down the tent, set Wallace's bedroll in the center of it, and rolled them together, so that the bundle could be tied to the bottom of the pack.

"We're ready, Carly," Jamie said.

Carly led the horses into the clearing, ropes tied to saddle horns so that they followed in a string.

Wallace scowled. "How the hell am I supposed to mount when my hands are behind me?"

Reaper smiled and pushed him toward one of the horses. When they stood beside it, Reaper grabbed Wallace by the belt and pitched him upward. Before Wallace fell over the other side, Reaper grabbed his leg and arm and turned him to face forward, and then guided his foot into the stirrup. "Any more questions?"

As Reaper walked away, his smile slipped, and he grimaced while he rubbed his lower back.

Carly shook her head. "We'll be back home in our own bed tonight. No excuses, Reaper," she sang.

"We about ready?" Cochise gritted out. If the women said they needed to take a trip to the woods, he might lose it. It would take most of the day to get back to the road. Calculating in his head, he figured he could be back in Bear Lodge, showered, and standing on Sammy's doorstep sometime before ten PM. And no, he wouldn't even consider waiting to see her until a polite time of morning.

"A little anxious to get home?" Jamie asked as she walked to her horse.

Cochise ground his teeth. "Been wearing these clothes for three days straight."

"So, you're anxious to get back to take a shower?" Lacey called out, laughing.

He gave both ladies the blackest scowl he could manage, which sent them into gales of laughter.

Sky stepped up beside him and clapped a hand on his shoulder, partially slapping the stiches that were nearly healed.

Cochise held back a wince, but just barely.

"Hope she's not on shift, buddy."

He didn't bother to pretend he didn't know who Sky was talking about. "Doesn't matter. I'll find her."

"Should have called her, buddy," Hook said, stepping up into the stirrup and swinging his leg over the saddle. He unknotted the rope tied to his saddle and clucked at his horse. Moving past Wallace, he reached for his horse's reins and led him away.

Cochise appreciated that Hook wasn't wasting time. He strode to his own horse, slid his rifle into its scabbard, and mounted.

"Can't believe how easy that capture was," Lacey

said. "Almost makes me embarrassed we couldn't find him all by ourselves."

Jamie whistled for Tessa, who flew to her side. "Maybe we should talk to the big boss about purchasing you a tracking dog. We could use another on the team."

As both women mounted their horses and rode away, he heard Lacey say, "Do you think he could be trained to sniff out bombs, too?"

Dagger groaned.

Cochise couldn't help it. For the first time in days, he smiled.

CHAPTER 9

BEFORE HE DROVE into Bear Lodge, Cochise swallowed his pride and called Brian.

After Brian stopped pretending that his laughter was a coughing fit, he called around to find out whether Office McCallister was on duty that night.

Thankfully, she was not. He hit his house first then had to ignore the bird that had nested in a corner of his living room ceiling after some other critter had torn through a screen window. He'd worry about "relocating" the nest later. He needed a shower.

Twenty minutes later, he was in his Expedition and heading to her apartment. Only, when he turned into her driveway, he realized he needed to do some groveling, so he turned around, found some flowers in the local supermarket, then plucked wilting blooms from the bouquet before he headed back.

He noted her truck was parked outside and girded himself for the coming confrontation.

Standing at her front door, he felt foolish. He wore his newest blue jeans, a blue Western shirt with pearl buttons that he'd never worn before, and his hair was scraped back in a rubber band. He was as presentable as he could be. So, why was he nervous?

Feeling as though he was getting ready to take a really tough shot, he drew a deep breath and waited for calm.

The door swung open, and he blinked in surprise.

Sammy stepped forward, and then gasped when she saw him there. "What the hell?" She pressed her hand against her chest.

So, he'd already blown step one. He thrust out the flowers, misjudged the distance, and slapped them against her chest. "Fuck."

Sammy stared at the flowers then glanced up into his face. A moment later, her lips twitched. Then she bent at the waist and began to laugh.

Heat spread across his cheeks. He wasn't quite certain what to do. She hadn't invited him in.

When she straightened, she met his gaze again, and then reached for his wrist and dragged him over the threshold. Once inside, she shut the door and settled her back against it. Her smile vanished, and one dark blonde brow arched. "It's been a while."

Cochise resisted the urge to tug at his too-tight collar. "When we got back to Eureka, Dagger and

Lacey called. They'd lost the trail of the man they were after. They needed the dog."

"They needed the dog..." Her other brow rose high.

He cleared his throat. "Jamie asked me to come along. Hook, too. Thought we'd knock it out in a day."

She folded her arms over her chest. "You couldn't call?"

Cochise didn't like her posture or her tone. He gave her a frown. "I didn't want to talk to you on a sat phone with an audience. Like I said, I thought I'd be back in a day or two. But then..." More heat suffused his face. "A horse stomped on the sat phone."

"Uh huh."

She didn't believe him? He almost blurted she could check with Hook, but he wasn't ten years old. Again, he held out the flowers. "These are for you."

She studied his face for a long moment then reached out a hand, taking her sweet time to accept the bouquet. "They're pretty." She straightened away from the door and walked toward her kitchen.

He trailed behind her, unsure about her mood. Sammy pulled a vase from a cupboard and filled it with water. Still silent, she cut the rubber band from around the bouquet and placed the flowers, one bloom at a time, into the vase. Again, taking her time.

Annoyed now, he reached for the remainder of the flowers, swiped them from her hand, and plunked them in the vase. "I have some things to say," he growled.

"Obviously."

Her tone was even, which confused him. Anger, he could handle. "Look, do you want me to go? I know I should have called. I didn't mean to wait so long. But I'll leave, seeing as you're pissed."

He rubbed his hand over his head frustrated and disappointed with how things were going. He'd thought they had a connection.

She moved toward her front door, and his shoulders sagged. Jesus, he hadn't been inside two minutes and she was showing him out.

But she turned the deadbolt, locking them inside. When she didn't turn around, he took a chance and stepped close behind her.

Sliding his hands around her waist, he bent and kissed her cheek. "I'm sorry," he said, his voice gruff.

"Me, too," she said softly. "But you surprised me. I'd decided today that you just weren't that into me."

He pulled her closer, so she could feel just how "into her" he wanted to be. "I should have called. I won't make that mistake again."

She tilted her head to the side. "That almost sounds like you plan to stick around."

Tired of talking to her without looking into her eyes, he gripped her shoulders and turned her. He moved closer, trapping her against the door, because he didn't want any distance between them when he said what he had to say.

"I know," he started slowly, "that we moved too fast. We didn't know each other well the first time we were together. I don't want you to think that because I didn't take time, that I'm unwilling to do so now."

"You want to slow this down?" she asked, a frown digging a shallow line between her brows.

"If you want—"

"I don't," she said quickly.

He drew another breath, because her quick response pleased him, but he wanted her to be sure. To think about what they could mean to each other. "But *if we did*, you'd learn to trust me."

She held still. "I see. If I'd known you better, or at least understood your intentions toward me, then I wouldn't have assumed you'd dumped me."

He nodded. Relieved he didn't have to explain, because the longer he stood close to her, the harder it was to concentrate. Her hair smelled of strawberries, and the supple waist he held tempted him to explore more of her sweet body.

Sammy's frown eased. "How about we take it slow...tomorrow," she whispered.

* * *

She knew the second he realized what she'd said. His black pupils dilated in his dark, dark eyes, and his nostrils flared. Those strong fingers gripping her waist began to squeeze. Following her desire, she raised her face to his.

He released her waist, cupped her cheeks between his palms, and kissed her. The moment their lips connected, she moaned and pressed her body against his. He gathered her closer, a hand clutching her hair, the other sliding down to her ass. When they broke apart, she pulled away and led him to her bedroom.

He flicked on every light as she stripped. Then he tossed away his own clothing, donned a condom, and strode toward her, his midnight eyes filled with wicked promises.

The moment she flipped back the covers on her bed, he lifted her and placed her in the center. When he came down over her, she sighed and began to slide her hands over his chest and arms, enjoying the warmth of his skin and the strength of the underlying muscles.

He kissed her cheek then moved lower, his tongue and lips conducting their own exploration as he made his way down her neck to her chest. When his mouth latched onto a nipple she sank her fingers in his hair and anchored him to her nipple.

Cochise sucked and flicked until the tip beaded against his tongue. Then he moved across to coax the other to blossom.

Again, he scooted downward, and her belly began to quiver. He traced her ribs, dove into her bellybutton, then bit gently at her skin as he moved lower, not stopping until he rested between her legs.

With his thumbs, he parted her folds and teased

her with long glides from the bottom to the top of her pussy, pausing over her hooded clit. With a scrape of a thumb, he exposed it, and then sucked against it, until she raised her knees and tilted her hips, begging silently for more.

Her head turned side to side; her mind floated away as he pleasured her. When his thick fingers entered her, she clenched her inner muscles and cried out.

But this wasn't how she wanted to come. She reached down and pulled his hair, forcing him to slide back up her body.

When he was poised above her, his hands braced on either side of her, she reached between their bodies and guided his cock inside her. She couldn't help crying out again as he thrust deep.

He paused. "Did I hurt you?"

"No," she said, trying to catch her breath. She was already panting. "It was the anticipation." She licked her lips. "Feels good."

He arched one dark brow. "Just good?"

She lifted her legs and gripped the sides of his hips. "It'll feel better when you move."

His lips twitched, but then he glanced down between their bodies, dragging her gaze along with his.

He began to move, his thick cock pulling out, glistening with her moisture. When he pushed in, she tightened her muscles around him.

"Damn, Sammy," he said, his jaw grinding, and stroked faster.

At first, they watched their bodies join and pull apart, a sight so incredibly erotic that she couldn't contain a moan. "More," she said, moving her legs to encircle him.

"Touch your tits," he said.

While he continued to give her deep strokes, she cupped her breasts and lifted them. Then she pinched and pulled on one nipple, while twisting the other. Her eyelids dipped, floating open then closed, because the pleasure was immense—his cock stroking, his dark eyes staring as she pleasured herself.

"Play with your clit."

She didn't mind his hoarse commands, because she knew she was the one in charge. She watched his face tighten and his nostrils flare as she wet her finger in her mouth, and then pulled up the top of her stretched folds to fondle the hard, red nubbin.

Suddenly, he straightened and forced her legs from his waist. Then he hooked his arms beneath her knees and raised her bottom from the bed. His gaze dropped to her pussy as he began to power into her, his thrusts hard and deep.

She resumed toggling her clit, until it grew so sensitive she couldn't take any more. She flung her arms wide and gripped the bedding, watching as every muscle in his arms and belly flexed and stretched.

Then he changed his motions, shortening his thrusts, grinding against her when he went deep. His gaze lifted to hers, and she saw the challenge in his eyes. She knew he was close, but that he'd hold back. For her.

"Harder," she gasped.

He bared his teeth and powered harder. Once, twice...

On the third hard stroke, she shouted, "Yes!"

He gave a muffled shout and followed her, losing rhythm as he drove deep. She felt the spasms deep inside her as he came. When he halted altogether, he rolled, one hand pressing on her ass to keep them connected. After stretching on top of him, she closed her legs to trap his cock inside her.

Sammy rubbed her cheek against his slick shoulder while she enjoyed the glides of his hands as they smoothed over her back and bottom. She nuzzled into his neck. "Cochise..."

"Yes, baby?"

"I think...I'm falling for you."

He pulled back his head to look at her. "You just think...?"

The humor in his voice relieved her. She hadn't scared him. "Um, actually, I know."

One corner of his mouth quirked. "Well, I'm damn sure I love you."

She blinked, and then a smile stretched her mouth. "So much for taking it slow."

His laughter jerked his chest. They both grew

quiet, but it was a comfortable silence as their breaths deepened and their heartbeats settled.

After a few minutes, Cochise lifted her chin, tilting it upward until their gazes met. "Just so you know, I have a house that needs some work, but if you're patient, I'll get it ready for both of us. There's room for Sheri, too."

Boy, he liked moving fast. But so did she. She wrinkled her nose. "I'm pretty handy with a hammer and a paint brush. I could help."

Cochise's gaze was steady as he nodded. "We could have a good life here, together."

She liked the sound of that. Settling again, she circled one flat brown nipple with a fingertip. "You know, my work schedule's four on, four off. If I picked up some part-time work, tracking skips, we might be able to spend more time together..."

His teeth gleamed brightly. "You mean, you want to be a bounty hunter?"

With a shrug, she said, "Not full-time, but it might be fun."

He sighed. "I'm sure Jamie would welcome you. She was already talking about offering Sheri a job in the office, helping Brian until she leaves for school."

"I have no doubt she'd be thrilled." She shook her head in wonder. Her life was about to change in so many ways.

In the distance, she heard the door slam. She froze and darted a glance at Cochise.

He looked at the open door.

"No time," she whispered.

They rolled apart, and she reached for the covers that were twisted under them. Just as she dragged a sheet up to cover them, Sheri was standing in her doorway.

"Hey, Sammy! I'm ho—" Her jaw dropped, and her gaze flicked from Cochise to Sammy.

"Um, you might have called first," Sammy said weakly.

Sheri screamed and rushed into the bedroom. She jumped onto the end of the bed, bouncing them all. "I can't believe it. I thought you weren't even interested in boys!"

Cochise choked and then began to laugh.

Sheri looked at him then back at her sister. "Oh my, he's cute without his clothes."

Sammy tossed a pillow at her sister. "Get out! We need to get dressed before we have this conversation."

Smiling slyly, her sister edged off the mattress and moved toward the door. "That's so not fair." With her hand on the doorknob, she gave her sister a prim smile. "I hope I don't have to talk to you about using condoms..."

Laughter followed her down the hallway.

* * *

When he was sure Sammy's sister was well away, Cochise rolled over Sammy, trapping her beneath him. "At least we know how your sister is going to take this new development."

Sammy smiled as she reached up and cupped his cheek. "I love you."

Cochise was pretty sure he'd never tire of hearing those words. He'd been alone and angry for far too long. As he gazed down into Sammy's laughing green eyes, his heart felt full, at peace. At last, he'd found a family to call his own.

Don't miss the next Montana Bounty Hunters book:
Hook!

ABOUT DELILAH DEVLIN

Delilah Devlin is a *New York Times* and *USA TODAY* bestselling author with a reputation for writing deliciously edgy stories with complex characters. She has published nearly two hundred stories in multiple genres and lengths, and she is published by Atria/Strebor, Avon, Berkley, Black Lace, Cleis Press, Ellora's Cave, Entangled, Grand Central, Harlequin Spice, HarperCollins: Mischief, Kensington, Montlake Romance, Running Press, and Samhain Publishing.

You can find Delilah all over the web:
WEBSITE
BLOG
TWITTER
FACEBOOK FAN PAGE
PINTEREST

Subscribe to her newsletter ***so you don't miss a thing!***

Or email her at: delilah@delilahdevlin.com

THE BOUNTY, PART 2

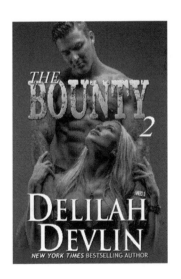

A female bounty hunter and her partner master the art of the takedown—on each other!

* * *

Note: This 6,000-word short story is intended to be dirty. Just sayin'. You've been warned!

* * *

Working for A+ Bounty Hunters was the most fun I'd ever had—out of bed, that is. Especially now that I was no longer encumbered by "training wheels." I'd proven myself to the agency's lead, Catch, and to my partner Bulldog. Sure, Bulldog still had certain rules he made me follow—like, he was always the first to enter a building where we knew we might face resistance, and that I'd better be ready for some sexy retribution if ever something I did scared him (yes, there were a few things that scared my big badass boyfriend!).

I think he knew I didn't mind his punishments, but it was our thing. The way we blew off steam and tension. Once the bad guy was in lockup, we'd find the first restroom, logging trail, or deserted alleyway and go at it like rabbits on steroids.

I liked our quick, hard fucks. Bulldog's fierce frowns and angry intensity always turned me on. Those fucks took off the edge until we made it back to our place for more leisurely play.

"Our" place was Bulldog's house deep in the woods. He'd invited me to move in a month ago. A formality since I'd been sleeping there every single night for two months already. But he was slow to trust. Slow to accept change. The fact he'd been attracted to me in the first place had annoyed the hell out of him. He didn't fuck his fellow hunters. But then again, A+ had never hired a "girl" before me. He'd been assigned as my trainer, but I hadn't been a very good student. I didn't stay where he put me and constantly ended up in the middle of some shit-storm takedown—bruised and cut but grinning. An ex-Army MP with combat experience, I wasn't a wuss. Something I made sure he knew from our very first bust.

He'd underestimated me. I'm five-feet-five and slender. He'd taken one look at my blonde hair and blue eyes and decided on the spot I was unsuited to the life. He'd even given me my nickname—Buttercup—thankfully, not adding the "princess" part, but everyone got his meaning. He hadn't expected me to last a day as his trainee, but I proved to be every bit as stubborn as he was.

Admitting he was wrong about me had set his teeth on edge, because he didn't want me working there, didn't want me anywhere near any danger. You see, Bulldog, at his heart, had a soft spot for women in general and an ingrained protective instinct towards those he cared about. And Bulldog cared about me but had yet to admit how deep that caring went.

As for my feelings…? I was head over heels, old-fashioned *besotted* with the dude. Everything I'd learned about him, everything he made me feel when he handled my body, told me I'd never experience the likes of Bulldog again. I wasn't willing to let what I felt, *or him*, go, because I knew I'd never find this again.

So, there you have it. Bulldog and I were still dancing around each other—working hard, playing harder—and because I feared that pushing for a declaration might cause him to react in stubborn opposition, I kept silent, bottling up the emotions roiling inside me. Was I being cowardly? Probably. But this life wasn't bad. I spent every waking and sleeping hour right beside him. If proximity bred affection, I hoped, in the end, he'd realize the reason he liked having me around was for more than my "great tits" and endless sex drive. But now wasn't the time to be thinking about sex...

I glanced out the window of Bulldog's Dodge Ram truck as he jogged back after speaking to a group of bikers who'd exited a dive bar in Bear Lodge, Montana, and let go a deep sigh. At six-feet-four and heavily muscled, the man shouldn't be able to move as lithely as a big cat. He came around the front of the truck and opened his door. A blast of frigid air accompanied him as he slid into the seat beside mine. He shot me a glance.

His expression rarely gave away his thoughts, but I'd learned to read his eyes. Right now, the crinkles at the sides were deeper. He was plenty satisfied with what he'd learned. "Well? Did his buddies give him up?"

"Yup."

Fucker. His smirk said he wasn't sharing without a little effort on my part.

I narrowed my eyes and tapped my foot on the floor. "Well?"

"Can't hold your pee for a second, can you?"

I waited as he hit the ignition button and pulled back into the street. We headed north out of town.

Bulldog snorted. "His club isn't happy with him. Said he'd broken their rules when he'd roughed up his girlfriend. She's a friend to the group."

"Meaning she's slept with a few of them."

He cleared his throat. "Anyway, he's holed up at a hunting cabin ten miles out. They even drew me a map." He pulled a dingy bar napkin from a pocket of his jacket and handed it to me. "Think you can navigate?"

I raised an eyebrow but didn't rise to his bait. He'd have to work harder to piss me off.

Ten miles down the road, dusk was settling in, creating deep shadows in the forest around us. I pointed toward what looked like a logging trail to the right. A narrow, cleared road with a dusting of snow that accentuated muddy ruts and potholes.

Bulldog passed it and drove a couple of hundred feet farther to a wide shoulder in the road and parked. We both climbed out of the crew cab. He circled to my side, opened the passenger door behind my seat, and pulled out our go bag. He handed me a vest, my web belt, and my handgun. As we both donned our gear, he began his short briefing. "Remember, this guy has no qualms about beating a woman. Keep clear of his fists. When we get to the cabin, let me do the recon." He handed me an earpiece then waited as I fitted it into my ear.

And then, as always, he gripped my upper arms and pulled me in for a quick kiss. "Stay safe," he said gruffly as he set me back.

I gave him a wide grin, just so he'd know much fun I thought this was.

He shook his head, but the corners of his mouth twitched.

And off we went, following the rough trail to the cabin that the directions scribbled on the napkin said was four hundred yards in beside a small stream. With me admiring Bulldog's broad shoulders and tight ass, I nearly stumbled a couple of times, because I was so busy noticing how good he looked I didn't see the potholes.

The cabin was exactly where the bikers had said we'd find it. "Boy, his buddies must be really pissed," I murmured.

"I'm going to circle around. You stay put until you hear from me."

I kept quiet. And still.

For about a minute.

A light shone between closed shutters, which meant someone was home. I raised my feet high and lowered them slowly, trying to make as little noise in the snow as I could.

"You're walking..." came Bulldog's voice, deadly and low.

"I'm moving my feet. They're cold."

"Dammit, Buttercup."

I ducked as I got closer to the cabin and kept my head below the windowsill. One quick dart upward, and I stared into the skinny slit. I couldn't see much, just a rickety table and an open beer can. I ducked down again. "Can't see if he's the one inside."

A string of whispered curses sounded in my ear. "Going around front. No back door. A window on the north and on your side. Stay at yours."

Like hell. With my back to the side of the cabin, I edged quietly toward the front of the cabin.

Three hard knocks sounded, followed by, "Fugitive Recovery Agent! Jeremy Bullock, come out with your hands up!"

I strained my ears, listening for sounds coming from inside the cabin then heard a huge crash as Bulldog kicked in the door.

Beside me, the shutters burst open and a booted foot appeared over the windowsill. "Got a runner," I whispered, as I edged back to the window.

"Goddammit, Jeremy, fucking get back inside that window!"

Jeremy tumbled to the ground then bounced back up.

I unclipped my telescoping night stick and jerked my hand to extend it.

Jeremy's head turned at the sound, but before he

could turn his body too, I swung out the stick and caught him behind the knees. Down he went.

"Oh, my fucking knee!"

A growl sounded behind me, and I glanced back to see Bulldog grip both sides of the window a second before he propelled himself through it.

Although I had a head start, he reached Jeremy first, flipping him to his belly and kneeling on his ass as he snapped handcuffs on his skinny wrists.

When he stood, Bulldog reached down and gripped Jeremy by the collar of his jacket to pull him to his feet.

Lord, I loved it when he got physical. All that manly power on display. Jeremy only limped a little as Bulldog propelled him back through the woods toward the truck.

Over his shoulder, Bulldog said, "Lock up the cabin. Make sure he didn't have a flame going. And be quick."

I didn't mind that he barked orders at me. Adrenaline was still spiking his system. When he came down, he'd be quiet. Blame it on me giving him another scare because I hadn't stayed where he wanted me to be. Twice.

I quickly went through the cabin, closing the window, turning off the propane heater. As I passed the cot in the back, I noted a stack of porn magazines, the topmost featuring a girl with wooden clothespins attached to her purpling nipples. *Ouch.* I wrinkled my nose as I let myself out of the cabin and pulled the door as far closed as I could in its splintered state.

Clothespins? Had to hurt.

* * *

Later, after we'd dropped off Jeremy and were heading home, Bulldog glanced across at me. "You're quiet. What's wrong?"

The man wasn't big on conversation. His words always got straight to the point. "Nothin'." I still had clothespins on my mind, and now I wished I'd used the toe of one of my boots to flip a few of the pages.

He grunted.

I smiled. His eyes were narrowing, and although we were only fifteen miles away from his place, I knew he was looking for a secluded spot. He flipped his turn signal and made a hard right. I guessed a spot behind a convenience store was private enough for what he had in mind.

As soon as he punched the button to kill the engine, he hopped out of the cab and circled the truck. With the passenger side facing a concrete retaining wall, and with no security lights illuminating the back of the store, he jerked open my door, grabbed my legs and swung them outside. Then he pushed me back against the console as he went to work getting me out of my pants.

"Hey, it's cold! What's this for?" I said, playing

my part. I had to resist or neither of us would have any fun. And Bulldog played his. Maybe, too well.

He'd gone silent. His hands moved with lightning speed, opening my belt, unzipping and dragging my pants to my thighs. Then he stepped up on the running board and grabbed my waist, forcing me to my belly. Feeling a flutter of alarm because my legs were constricted, and he still hadn't said a word, I gasped as he pulled me outside, fitted my boots to the running board then slipped his hands between my legs. When he'd managed to get his own pants down, I'd never know, but suddenly, his cock was pushing against my pussy, no searching or shimmying in, just a straight thrust that "popped" into place once he'd pushed through my lips.

I realized he was half-standing on the running board, too, his legs spread wide around mine. He shoved his hands beneath me, working them under my shirt and bra until he was cupping my breasts, his large hands squeezing as he pumped inside me.

This wasn't a comfortable fuck—friction built quickly because he rubbed through my pussy lips and slapped my bottom with every thrust, but my clit was being neglected, and I had no way of angling my body to make sure he struck it at least now and then.

And then he pinched my nipples, squeezing the tips between his thumbs and middle fingers, hard. I was reminded of that pinup's purple nipples, and instantly, I arched. "Harder!"

He stroked harder, causing the truck to squeak and rattle.

"No, my tits!"

His fingernails dug into the tender bits, and I flew, letting loose a breathy screech.

Two more pumps, and Bulldog emptied himself inside me.

Then as though nothing had happened, he backed away. I heard the sounds of him putting his clothing back together then he picked me up and turned me to sit in my seat—my bare ass on cold leather—and buckled me in.

His face still set in tight lines, he marched around the cab and climbed into the driver's seat. He didn't spare me a glance—me, with my pussy leaking all over his leather and starting to shiver because now that the heat of the moment had passed, I was fucking freezing.

I didn't dare complain as he backed out of the dark space and onto the road.

Fifteen minutes later, he tapped his garage opener and drove inside. "Don't move."

I watched as he entered the mud room just off the kitchen then reappeared a minute later, his hand cupped around something. He opened my door and waited as I slid my legs toward the opening. "Hold these."

I held open my hand, and he deposited two ancient-looking wooden clothespins on my palm. My nipples sprang, and I glanced up at Bulldog's face.

His eyelids were sleepy-looking, his sexy look. His jaw was hard. "I saw the magazine, too," he said. "It's why I had you go back inside. I didn't give a fuck if the place burned down."

"So, back there, you weren't really mad..."

"You didn't tell me what was wrong. I've told you before—you want something, you just tell me."

I licked my lips and stared down at the clothes-pins. "They'll hurt."

"And we know you like a little pain." He flicked a finger at one of my spiked nipples.

Even through the shirt, the sting shot a dart of lust straight to my pussy.

I gave a little gasp. "If it's too much?"

"Trust me?"

"Always," I whispered. Me trusting him had never been a problem.

Giving me no more warning than that, he gripped my shoulders and pulled me forward. Then he hefted me over one of his brawny shoulders. As he strode through the house, I curled my fingers tightly around those clothespins. At any point, I could have dropped them. He wouldn't have said a word.

Once inside the bedroom, he set me on my feet. When he began stripping, I knew I better not be wearing a stitch by the time he finished. I tossed the pins toward the bed and removed everything.

He lifted his chin toward the mattress, and I reached out to pull back the coverlet. I tossed it to the end of the bed then crawled into the middle, kneeling there with my hands on my thighs and my engorged nipples impudently lifted. A tremor rippled through me as my gaze strayed toward the pins.

Now, Bulldog had used clamps before. Cute ones with little bells that dangled and rang every time I quivered or jerked. But they'd been covered with rubber and could be adjusted to my tolerance for pressure.

"Look at me."

I blew out a breath between my pursed lips and lifted my gaze. Lord, even after all these months, he took my breath away.

It wasn't that he was particularly handsome. His features were too rugged—his nose crooked, his jaw hard. His body was a study of grayscale tats cloaking his massively muscled chest and arms. Just the thought of the power he delivered with his hard ass and thighs when he fucked made me wet.

He climbed onto the mattress on his knees and swiped up the clothespins. "Sure about this?"

I swallowed hard. My nipples were already spiked, already sensitive from the way he'd pinched them earlier, but I gave a nod. Then I watched as he plucked one nipple, pinching around the base to extend the tip. He squeezed a clothespin, then opened it wide around the tip and slowly let it close. At first, the sting felt familiar, no big deal, but my eyes widened as he let it go.

"Too much?"

With the liquid pooling between my legs, my body didn't seem to think so. "No."

He released it altogether, and I hissed air between my teeth. "*Fuck, fuck, fuck...*"

Staring downward, at the one nipple with the tip protruding from the pin, I drew short breaths until the stinging eased.

Bulldog toggled the tip, and I closed my eyes. The pain and the stimulation felt divine.

"Ready for the next?"

This time my nod was quicker. Again, I watched his big fingers pinch my nipple to extend the tip, then clamp it, slowly releasing the full pressure. When he toggled it, my jaw dropped. "Bulldog..."

"Chris," he whispered.

He liked it when I used his real name during sex.

"Chrissss..."

"Get on your knees. Watch yourself in the mirror."

I crawled onto my hands and knees and then raised my head. The clothespins attached to my nipples looked obscene.

Bulldog crawled behind me and placed his hands atop my ass.

I lowered my chest until my tips were inches from the mattress but my ass was high.

"What did I tell you to do at the cabin?" he muttered, stirring his hands atop my skin, warming it.

Oh, goody! He hadn't forgotten. "I didn't stay where you told me to."

He raised a hand and slapped it downward on my right cheek. The blow jerked me, made my breasts jiggle, and the pins tighten—or maybe it was blood rushing to the tips to further engorge them. Didn't matter, it stung. Felt fucking amazing.

"You knew I had him. The cabin was tiny. I was on his ass, but you had to confront him."

I met his gaze in the mirror and lifted my chin. "I know. I was thinking about later. What you'd do..."

Again, he swatted—this time the other side. "I had him. You didn't have to risk getting hurt."

"I wasn't in the least bit of danger from that skinny shit—"

Whack!

"Fucker, that hurt!"

Whack!

I groaned and leaned my head against the coverlet as he popped me again and again—stinging slaps, thuddy pats—and all the while my breasts shivered, and the pins squeezed tighter until I was a mass of burning need. My ass was on fire, but my pussy convulsed, releasing a stream of fluid that wet my bare mound.

And then he cupped me, fingers sliding inside to swirl. His thumb caressing my clit. His hand fell away, and I braced. The next slap, and the next, landed against my cunt.

I gave a tiny, kittenish mew. I could come so easily. If only he'd let me.

"Raise your head. I want to see your tits."

141

My back sank as I lifted my head. In the mirror, my breasts looked larger, the clothespins almost comical.

Bulldog crawled closer, and his thighs flanked mine. He pushed down my ass and pressed his cock against my folds. With a single, straight thrust, he rushed inside me.

My expression, even to me, was desperate. My eyes glittered with unshed tears. My body shivered hard.

Bulldog reached around me, unclipped the pins, and cupped my breasts, his large hands nearly encompassing the globes. Then he stroked, moving in and out, his gaze locked with mine in the mirror, watching my face as an agony of sensations rocked through me.

The sudden rush of blood to my nipples felt cold, until he spread his fingers and squeezed the tips between them. They were so engorged they remained visible as he massaged. Then his thrusts grew harder, sharper, and I had to grip the mattress and reset my knees to keep from falling forward.

My gaze remained glued on him. His features tightened, grew scarily feral. His lips peeled away from his teeth. His sexy snarl fascinated me. As did the play of muscles, bulging, growing more defined as sweat built.

Suddenly, he pushed me forward, his cock sliding free. I rolled and scooted away, forcing him to chase me. A hand clamped around my ankle, and then he crawled over me, again, like a big cat, his mouth dipping to my skin. His tongue lashed, trailing upward, flicking my clit. He bit my mound, my belly, then paused at my breasts.

"Too much!" I gasped as his lips closed around my ravaged nipple.

But he gave tender laps of his tongue and gently sucked the tip.

My legs moved restlessly; my belly undulated. I needed him inside me. Needed him to finish this. *Needed him to say he loved me...*

He plied the other breast with tender strokes and sucks, but I was whimpering now with need.

At last, he moved upward and rested on his elbows. He brushed hair from my sweaty face and bent to kiss my mouth. A soft kiss. Lovely, because it was so rare.

He lowered his chest and reached back to snag my knees, bringing them upward, forcing my legs higher until they pressed against my chest.

His glance cut to my breast, hidden now. Without being told, I reached into the space between them and brought my breasts out, squished as they were.

"I love your tits."

"Because they're big?" I gasped.

He gave a savage shake of his head. "Because they never lie."

"I never lie, Chris."

"You also never obey."

I arched an eyebrow. "And yet we're here."

"Hold your legs." When I clutched the backs of my knees, he reared backward and cupped my ass, holding it still as he prodded my opening.

The feel of his blunt round knob entering me again was so exquisite, I bit my lower lip to keep from crying out.

When he leaned over me again, he braced on his hands and powered hard, his hips slapping, grinding. He thrust so deep and hard my breaths came in ragged gusts. When he quickened the motions, I watched enthralled as his eyes lost focus and his mouth opened. A long, stretched rumble accompanied the hot spurts of come that filled my channel.

I reached for his face, pulled him nearer, then lifted my head to kiss him. "I'm soaked inside. Flood-ed," I whispered.

"Sorry," he gritted out, still quivering in the aftermath.

I rubbed my cheek against his sweaty one. "Hmmm. Thought that was the punishment." I was teasing, because he never left me wanting.

He rested his head on the pillow beside mine for a long moment until I made a wheezing sound.

He moved back, reluctance in his grimace as he pulled free and let me lower my legs. Then his gaze sharpened. He reached for two pillows. "Lift your ass."

I shook my head. "That really will be too much,"

I whispered. I knew, because his oral always blew my mind.

But his gaze only narrowed, so I lifted my ass and let him shove two pillows beneath it. While he arranged my thighs just so, I cupped my breasts out of a need to comfort myself.

Then he was there, his face between my legs, his mouth and tongue flicking, toggling, biting. But he never touched my clit. My nude outer lips were sucked until they swelled. My inner lips were mouthed and tugged until I felt the electricity arc all the way to my toes. All the while my clit hardened, the hood sliding slowly away, leaving the nubbin exposed to the cool air. The lightest touch would set me off—but that was not his intention. And I didn't dare give in to the urge to fly—not without his okay, because he took pride in stripping me down to a quivering, slobbering mess. *Fucker.*

Not that I didn't love every minute of his relentless torture. My belly was already shivering, my thighs jerking every time he surprised me with flick or flutter. When his thumb entered my ass, my shoulders rolled off the bed. "Chris!"

That came out a little too high-pitched for my pride's sake, but I had no control. My fingers clipped my nipples and jiggled my breasts—a distraction from the fact his fingers were finding their way inside my other hole, and he was fucking them in and out.

At last, he raked a calloused thumb across my naked clit, and I shouted.

"Not yet," he warned.

My head thrashed, and I let go of my breasts to reach for his head. I sank my nails into his golden-brown hair and raked his scalp.

Bulldog spit on my clit, then using his thumb and forefinger, he squeezed around the base, forcing it outward like a little penis. Then he wagged his flattened tongue across the tip.

My hips jumped at the motions. Heat spread outward from my pussy, cramping my womb, causing my nipples to tingle.

When he spit again, and then began to milk my clit, jerking it off with tiny, pinching rubs, I raised my legs into the air and let them fall open, toes pointed. I was unable to breathe, to speak. I reached out my arms and let them fall against the mattress, surrendering everything. The need centered on that tiny spot was so intense it was painful. So beautiful, I began to cry.

And then he latched his lips around my clit and sucked, his fingers fucking my pussy and my ass.

I sobbed.

"Now, baby. Come now."

I breathed in then screamed, pleasure unraveling inside me. Waves of lush heat lapped over me. My breath returned in quivering inhalations, and I lay limp against the humid sheets.

I realized Bulldog's arms surrounded me, and I turned to nuzzle against his skin, exhausted but also triumphant. As though I'd climbed Everest and survived.

Bulldog's hand smoothed over my back and hip. His breathing was even. He was waiting for me to recover. For what? To talk? I doubted it. For our next round of sex? God, I wasn't sure my heart could take it.

My eyes were closed, but I felt his fingers wipe away the tears that had leaked as I'd come undone.

Wrinkling my nose, I opened my eyes and met his blue gaze. "That was..." How to describe it? There wasn't a word big enough to encompass what I felt. I shook my head and smiled.

"Buttercup," he whispered.

I liked my name. Liked that he'd given it to me. On his lips, it was becoming an endearment—at least, to me. "Chris." I placed my hand on his chest over his heart. It thudded against my palm—slow and steady.

"I like this."

Like? I couldn't help but sigh in disappointment.

His hand cupped my breast, his thumb hovering over one tender peak. "You okay?"

"A little sore."

"I won't use them again."

"Okay." I hated how awkward our words were becoming. I knew what to say when we were clothed. When we fucked. But never in these intimate moments.

"Fuck."

I glanced up again. His brows were furrowed.

"I like this."

"So you already said."

His mouth thinned. "I want you to stay."

"Already settled. My things are all here now."

"I mean...for good."

Okay, so that was different. A little less vague. Was now the time to push? I eased over his body. His cock was semi-flaccid, beginning to stir. I clamped it between my thighs as I lay over him. Just to get his attention. "I'll stay, but I have to know..."

His expression gave away nothing of what he was thinking. It was neutral, but his eyes... Was that glacial blue thawing?

"I..." Fuck, I had to say it. My body tightened, because I was scared. His cock, reacting to the pressure, was filling, getting thicker between us. "I love you," I blurted. And then I blushed—heat filling my cheeks.

His chest billowed as he drew a deep breath, and then lowered as he let it go. "I know."

He knows? And... His silence enraged me. "You fucker."

A smirk edged up one side of his mouth, and he held my hips as I tried to slide off his body. With an upward push, his cock dropped between my legs. He probed my entrance then slowly slid me down his hot, thick shaft.

Now pinned to his body, I wasn't through being mad. I shoved against his chest and tried to pull my knees up along his side, but he held me firmly in place.

"Stop."

His monosyllabic vocabulary wasn't sexy now. "*You* stop. Let me go." The last thing I wanted to do was start crying, or worse, begging for him to tell me what I needed to hear.

I loved him. Every ornery part of him—his bad moods, his bossiness, his strength. God, I loved how he handled me. Even now, forcing me up and down his cock while he held my gaze, not letting me look away as my face began to crumple. "Fuck you."

He rolled until he was on top then flexed his hips. My already friction-burned channel itched then grew wet. Soon, I was raising my hips to slam against his, my stubbornness and anger reasserting. I lifted my chin and fucked him while he fucked me.

However, getting us both off wasn't on his agenda. As soon as I grew wet and responsive, he closed my legs with his and clamped them tight. Resting on his elbows, his chest still kept my upper body wedged against the mattress.

"Ready to listen?" he whispered.

No, no, no. I shook my head. I shouldn't have pushed. If he told me anything less than what I craved hearing, I'd be crushed. Kind of like my body was right now.

"Tough. I didn't want you as a partner."

My glance fell away. "A sentiment you made known on day one."

149

"Shut up."

I frowned and pushed out my lower lip.

"I knew fucking you was off-limits, but you pushed every one of my buttons."

Seriously, you're going to blame me for the fact you can't keep your dick to yourself? Because I couldn't tell him in words, I bugged my eyes.

"Stop," he said, his voice softer.

I drew a deep, ragged breath and eased my frown. His gentleness could signal that this conversation was about to go one of two ways. I didn't want to hear, so I thought instead about the fact his cock was pulsing inside me. I squeezed my pussy around his thickness, which earned me a grunt.

"Buttercup."

"Pansy." I gritted my teeth, daring for him to laugh at my real name. Buttercup was a much better name for a badass bounty hunter.

His mouth twitched. "Buttercup," he said, his eyes narrowing. "I gave you that name because it pleases me....and someday, I'll give you another..."

That last bit, whispered so softly I wondered if I'd heard him right, had me blinking, and then searching his gaze. "So, when you said you wanted me to stay..."

"I meant forever. You're mine."

So, maybe he hadn't said the L-word, but I wasn't going to quibble. He liked *this*. *Us*. I did, too. My breathing deepened. My upset faded.

Satisfied, for now, I dragged a fingertip from his

shoulder to his small brown nipple. "Wanna try them?" I gave the tiny tip a pinch.

Bulldog growled and pushed his cock deeper.

"You know, that would work better if I could actually open my legs..."

"Your mouth never stops."

"Not true," I drawled, invitation in my eyes.

In a single blink, he pulled free then crawled upward over my body. Holding onto the headboard, he waited as I fisted his cock then opened to let him inside my mouth.

I loved giving him head. It was the only time I felt as though he made himself vulnerable to me. After all, I had his goodies in my hands, his cock between my teeth. I liked reminding him of those facts. Like now. As I tugged his balls and scraped my teeth down his length, I gazed upward into his eyes.

Sucking on him was sexy and comforting. An acknowledgement of his masculinity. An intimacy I bestowed upon the only man I craved to submit to. Taking him deeper was a challenge, because there was so much of him, and soon my jaws began to ache. I released his balls and slid a finger along the crease of his ass.

"Hell no," he muttered and pulled free. Then he gripped his cock around the base.

Not willing to give in so easily, I mouthed his balls, rubbing my tongue on one.

His head fell back. "I want to fuck your mouth and your cunt."

I scooted a few inches downward and fluttered my tongue against the spot right behind his balls.

"Jesus." He swung back his leg and knelt on his haunches, his cock still clutched in his big fist.

I reached for the clothespins, and then made a big show of attaching them to my tits, wincing and gasping as they closed. Then I sat on the edge of the bed and squeezed my breasts together with my hands. "Put it here," I said, then parted my breasts.

With his gaze glued to my tits, he rasped, "I won't last a second."

"Good. My tits hurt."

As it turned out, I sat too high, so we moved to the armchair. I settled on the edge as he bent his knees and gripped the arms. I licked him up and down to lubricate him, then pushed my chest toward him, and enclosed his cock between my breasts. He fucked my boobs, jerking up and down, his gaze on those damn pins and my purpling nipples. I guessed that the clothespins would be stashed in the bottom of one of my drawers for special occasions or for apology-sex. He sure liked the way they looked.

I bent my head and stuck out my tongue, licking him at the top of every stroke.

"Ah, Jesus, fuck," he ground out.

I knew he was close when he started cussing in triplicate. To increase the sensory detail, I squeezed him harder and bent my head to capture his head with my lips, sucking and popping when he withdrew.

"Now!"

I tossed back my head and felt hot come splash against my throat. I let go of my tits and unclipped the pins to let him rub more cream over my nipples. When he finished, he went to his knees and gobbled on my nipples while he fingered me.

Soon, I leaned back and lifted my legs over his shoulders, content to let him take me.

The phone rang on the night stand. His head lifted, his gaze meeting mine.

"Answer it," I said. So, we had a job, and I'd have to wait for my pleasure. But I'd get to watch my man in action again.

He picked up the phone and swiped the screen. I could hear Catch on the other end. We had another asshole running for the border. No time to lose.

"We've got this," Bulldog said.

When he hung up, I expected him to pull me up and turn me to the shower. Instead, he pushed two fingers into my ass. "Gotta hurry."

For him, my pleasure was as high a priority as any $10,000 bounty. Had to be love.